# Kitten MATH 2

a purr-fectly adorable fun math workbook

by Kelli Pearson

Copyright © 2025 Kelli Pearson

All rights reserved. No part of this book may be reproduced
or used in any manner without the prior written permission of
the copyright owner, except for the use of
brief quotations in a book review.

To request permissions, contact the publisher at kelli@artfulmath.com.

978-0-9855725-7-0

Cover art by Tjarda Borsboom
KASourGrape font by Kaitlynn Albani

Brain Spark Publishing
P.O. Box 1
Cupertino, CA 95015

https://artfulmath.com

for my dad,

the best kitty grandpa ever!

# TABLE OF CONTENTS

**Introduction** — 1
"PLEEEEASE, CAN WE GET A KITTEN??"

**Kittens Come Home** — 4
ADDING MANY NUMBERS, MULTIPLICATION

**Kittens Settle In** — 14
ADDING AND ROUNDING DECIMALS

**Get to Know Your Kittens** — 24
VENN, INTEGERS, MULTIPLICATION, 50% OFF, MONEY

**Hungry Kittens** — 36
MULTIPLICATION, PERCENTS, INTEGERS, FRACTIONS

**Life with Kittens** — 46
FRACTIONS, ELAPSED TIME, MEASUREMENT CONVERSION

**Design the Purr-fect Home for Kittens** — 54
ADDING AND SUBTRACTING DECIMALS, BUDGETING

**Working with Kittens** — 64
DECIMALS, ELAPSED TIME, ADD & MULTIPLY MONEY

**Happy Birthday, Kittens!** — 74
ELAPSED TIME, ADDING TIME, COORDINATE PAIRS, MONEY

**Let's Start a Kitten Club** — 82
POUNDS/OUNCES, SYMMETRY, AVERAGES, PROPORTION

**Answer Key** — 98

**Game Boards** — 104

**Certificate of Achievement** — 124

# There is MATH in this book!

I know, with a name like "Kitten Math" that probably isn't much of a surprise, but I thought I should warn you anyway.

**If you're usually NOT a math person, you'll be happy to know that math is a lot more fun with kittens. I mean, isn't EVERYTHING more fun with kittens??**

## Stuff you should know…

**You are not SUPPOSED to be good at all the math in this book.**

Not knowing and then finding out is called "learning".

Learning is the point.

**You can go SLOW and still be good at math.**

Take your time. Look closely. Think and figure things out. This is way more important than reciting math facts like a robot.

**NO FAIR giving up and saying you're bad at math.**

To get good at math, you have to make mistakes and keep trying—over and over again. That's how it works.

## What to do if you don't know how to do the math…

- Tell yourself, "**I don't know this yet… but I can learn it.**"
- **Take your time** and see if you can figure it out on your own.
- **Ask someone** to explain it to you.
- **Look at the answer key**, then see if you can get that answer on your own.
- If you're still unsure, **skip it and come back later.**

The most important thing is to have fun. Kittens are the BEST way to learn math!

# This book comes with online goodies

Kitten Math 2 comes with a free fun bonus pack of **adorable kitten videos, fun cat math and kitty art activities, cute progress chart, and more.**

You can also print all the **game boards, certificate, and cut-outs** from the book, so you don't have to cut the pages of your actual book.

—> Get all your Kitten Math bonuses at  artfulmath.com/kitten2-goodies

**Are you ready to meet your adorable kittens?** Let's go!

# "Pleeeease, can we get a kitten?"

**You've been begging for a kitten FOREVER.**

Every time you see their tiny, adorable, squishy faces, you feel like your heart just might explode with love!

They are just so cute!

"I'll clean the litter box **every single day**," you promise your parents.

"It will **teach me RESPONSIBILITY**!" you say. (That's sure to convince them!)

"**Please please please please please please pleeeeeeeease?**"

And then—a miracle happens! **Your parents say 'yes'!!!**

**Even better, they're talking about getting TWO kittens!**

(A vet told them that kittens are happier and better behaved when they have a friend. You LOVE that vet.)

You immediately start daydreaming about what your kittens will look like, the adorable & funny things they'll do all day, and **how awesome it will be to snuggle with their fluffy little bodies in bed at night.**

**You're going to be the ABSOLUTE BEST CAT PARENT EVER.**

You want to learn everything you can about how to keep your kittens healthy and happy.

**By the time you finish Kitten Math 2, you'll be an expert at taking care of growing kittens—and you'll know lots more math, too!**

# KITTENS COME HOME

A Visit to the Shelter

Why Adopt from a Shelter?

What Kind of Kittens Do You Want?

Picking Out Your Kittens

Kitten Name Math Code

# A VISIT TO THE SHELTER

"Let's stop by the animal shelter," dad says, "and let's take a look around."
You jump up and down! Could you really be getting a kitten—or even TWO kittens—today?

At the shelter, you talk with someone about adopting kittens. **Write your side of the conversation.**

**SHELTER WORKER**

> It's great you are thinking about adopting! Why do you want to adopt a kitten?

**YOU**

> _____

**SHELTER WORKER**

> You know, it's actually better to adopt TWO kittens so they can have a friend. How would you feel about that?

**YOU**

> _____

**SHELTER WORKER**

> What are some questions you have about taking care of kittens? What do you want to learn more about?

**YOU**

> _____

# WHY ADOPT FROM A SHELTER?

The shelter worker is so glad you want to rescue a kitten!

**"There are too many kittens being born in the streets,"** she says.
She explains how many kittens just **one female cat** can have in one year:

> One litter of kittens has an average of **5 kittens.**
> One mama cat can give birth to **3 litters per year.**

How many kittens could **one mama cat** give birth to in **one year**? _____

Imagine that nine of those kittens are female. **Mama Cat + 9 kittens = 10 cats**

How many kittens could **10 female cats** have in just **one year**? _____

How many kittens could **10 cats** have in **five years**? _____

That's a lot of kittens! And remember, all their female kittens are having kittens too. 😲
(Did you know that kittens can get pregnant as young as FOUR MONTHS OLD??)

**Now you are even more glad you adopted your kittens from a shelter.** There's no reason to buy kittens from a breeder, when there are so many on the street who are needing homes.

**What could you tell people to make this situation better?**

- ☐ Always get kittens spayed and neutered (surgery to not have babies).
- ☐ Adopt rescues from a shelter or foster home.
- ☐ Volunteer at local animal shelters and help get kittens adopted.
- ☐ Other: _____

The cats and kittens in the shelter are all shapes and sizes. It's sad to see them in cages, which makes you even more glad you'll be able to give TWO kitties a forever home!

**SHELTER WORKER:** It's so great that you are thinking about adopting TWO kittens!

**YOU:** I heard it's better to adopt two kittens, instead of just one. Is that true?

**SHELTER WORKER:** Oh yes, it's much better to adopt two kittens together. They play together, sleep together, and even teach each other not to bite or scratch! Are you looking for a particular age of kittens?

**YOU:** I'm thinking 8 weeks old? I saw a video that said that's a good age to adopt.

**SHELTER WORKER:** Yes, 8 weeks old is a great age to adopt. They are small and cute at that age, but you should know kittens are a lot of work. Are you ready for that?

**YOU:** Yes! I'm learning literally everything I can about kittens. I'll clean the litter box, play with them, pet them, give them the best food, brush them....

**SHELTER WORKER:** (laughing) Ok, ok! Those kittens will be so lucky to have you. Here we are at the kitten cages. Take a look around, and let me know which ones you like best!

# WHAT KIND OF KITTENS DO YOU WANT?

You notice that some kittens are quiet and calm, while others are wild and crazy! What personality traits are you looking for?

**Circle a number to show the traits you're looking for in each kitten.**

## Kitten 1

10 — 15 — 20
social and loud, meows a lot / a quiet kitten with big purrs

10 — 15 — 20
super playful, always running around / watchful and cuddly

10 — 15 — 20
funny, silly, mischievous / calm, sweet, and well behaved

10 — 15 — 20
brave, adventurous, a little crazy / a bit shy, but super smart

10 — 15 — 20
likes to sleep in the same room as you / likes to sleep right on top of you

Score ☐

## Kitten 2

10 — 15 — 20
social and loud, meows a lot / a quiet kitten with big purrs

10 — 15 — 20
super playful, always running around / watchful and cuddly

10 — 15 — 20
funny, silly, mischievous / calm, sweet, and well behaved

10 — 15 — 20
brave, adventurous, a little crazy / a bit shy, but super smart

10 — 15 — 20
likes to sleep in the same room as you / likes to sleep right on top of you

Score ☐

**Add the score for each kitten. Then find their result below.**

**85–100 points:** This is a **calm, sweet** lap kitty—the purr-fect quiet companion

**70–80 points:** This kitten is a little spicy, with a **great mix of cuddles and play**

**50–65 points:** This is a **wild and crazy,** mischievous kitten who always makes you laugh

# PICK OUT YOUR KITTENS

You've narrowed it down to a group of kittens who are bonded with each other. "Mom, dad, I've made up my mind!" you say. "Come quick! Can I show you my two favorites?"

Mom laughs and says, **"Yes, show me which two kittens you have in mind!"**

**Which two kittens will you bring home?** Write their numbers: _____ and _____

Your kittens are 8 weeks old today. **When was their birthday?** _____

Your kittens have learned 2 new things about the world each day they've been alive. How many things have they learned so far? _____

Write one new thing they've learned: _____

**What will you name your two perfect kittens?** Draw a picture of each one. Write about their personalities, quirks, and what you already love about them.

NAME: _____  ☐ male  ☐ female

| PICTURE | ABOUT |
|---|---|
|  | _____<br>_____<br>_____<br>_____<br>_____<br>_____<br>_____<br>_____<br>_____<br>_____ |

NAME: _____  ☐ male  ☐ female

| PICTURE | ABOUT |
|---|---|
|  | _____<br>_____<br>_____<br>_____<br>_____<br>_____<br>_____<br>_____<br>_____<br>_____ |

# KITTEN NAME MATH CODE

Let's play a game with your kittens' names! Here is a backwards number code. Each letter is worth money: A = $26, B = $25, etc.

| A | B | C | D | E | F | G | H | I | J | K | L | M | N |
|---|---|---|---|---|---|---|---|---|---|---|---|---|---|
| 26 | 25 | 24 | 23 | 22 | 21 | 20 | 19 | 18 | 17 | 16 | 15 | 14 | 13 |

| O | P | Q | R | S | T | U | V | W | X | Y | Z |
|---|---|---|---|---|---|---|---|---|---|---|---|
| 12 | 11 | 10 | 9 | 8 | 7 | 6 | 5 | 4 | 3 | 2 | 1 |

How much are your kittens' names worth? Add the numbers to find out!

Kitten 1 name: _____     $_____

Kitten 2 name: _____     $_____

How much are both kittens' names added together?  $_____

Here are some cute kitten nicknames. Add them up and write their totals in the boxes. Which nickname is worth the most? _____

☐ Boo Boo    ☐ Peanut    ☐ Squishy    ☐ Sweetie Pie

What's another nickname you might call your kittens?

Nickname: _____     $_____

Think of a kitten name or nickname that is close to $120. How close can you get?

Name: _____     $_____

# POUNCE GAME

  2-3 players

  paper and pencil

1. Write the numbers 1 to 20 in a line to make your game board.

2. Start off the game by crossing off any two numbers.

3. Add, subtract, multiply, or divide those two numbers to equal another number on the game board that is not crossed off yet.

4. Circle the answer to your math problem.

1 (2) 3 4 5 6 ~~7~~ 8 9 10 11 12 13 ~~14~~ 15 16 17 18 19 20

$14 \div 7 = 2$

5. The next player uses **the circled number and one other number** to make a new math problem.

6. Cross off those two numbers. Circle the answer on the game board.

1 ~~(2)~~ 3 4 5 6 ~~7~~ 8 ~~9~~ 10 11 12 13 ~~14~~ 15 16 17 (18) 19 20

$2 \times 9 = 18$

7. Keep playing, "pouncing" from one number to another until you can't make any more moves. (If you get stuck, you can ask other players for help.)

8. The last player to circle a number wins!

 *Watch a video showing how to play this game at **artfulmath.com/kitten2-goodies**

# KITTENS SETTLE IN

**Buying Kitten Supplies**

**Kitten Proof Your Home**

**Keeping Kittens Safe from Danger**

**Sharing Responsibilities**

# BUYING KITTEN SUPPLIES

**Hooray, your kittens are home!** For now, they are in the bathroom—a quiet place where they can settle in. While they are resting, you head to the pet store to get kitten supplies.

At the pet store, you ask so many questions: How many litter boxes do we need? How many toys should we get? How do I stop kittens from chewing on my phone charger?

You took notes so you would remember what to do. **Read your notes below, then look through the catalog on the following pages and put a check ✓ by the things you'll need to buy.**

YOUR NOTES

We need one litter box per cat, plus one more.

Get BIG litter boxes so we don't have to get new ones later.

Also, get a LITTER MAT so kittens don't track litter and dirty paws all over the house (and my bed)!

CAT WATER FOUNTAIN gets cats to drink more water.

Get CORD COVERS so kittens can't chew on phone cords!

LITTER GENIE is a non-stinky trash can to put by litter box.

DEFINITELY NEED:

litter box, litter   nail clippers
food dishes         collar
wet & dry food      cat carrier
cord protectors

GOOD TO HAVE:

water fountain   treats!
litter mat       probiotic
Litter Genie     food covers
cat brush (long-haired cats)

# KITTEN LOVE  PET STORE CATALOG

**Kitten Food Variety Pack**

Healthy food specially formulated for kittens. Pack of 24.

$55.99

**Chicken Kibble for Cats**

Tasty chicken and egg dry food recipe for cats and kittens. 6 pounds.

$27.95

**Cat Probiotics**

Soothes upset tummies and helps cats adjust to new foods. 30 packs.

$25.99

**Cat Food Dishes (2)**

Set of 2 ceramic food dishes with cute kitty faces.

$12.98

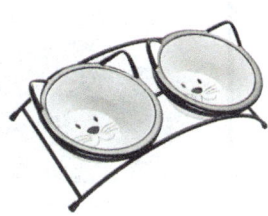

**Raised Cat Dish Set**

2 adorable cat-shaped dishes, raised for more comfortable eating.

$17.97

**Water Bowls (2)**

Deep, stainless steel bowls with non-slip bottoms. Quantity: 2

$8.99

**Drinking Water Fountain**

Stainless steel cat water fountain plugs into wall.

$29.99

**Waterfall Cat Fountain**

Easy-to-clean, cordless fountain holds a week's worth of water.

$31.95

**Chicken Baby Food**

Cats & kittens' favorite treat! Great for picky eaters. Includes 16 jars.

$23.99

**Tube Cat Treats**

50 squeezable cat treats in 5 irresistible flavors.

$31.97

**Canned Food Covers**

Keep leftover canned food fresh with four stretchable covers.

$4.99

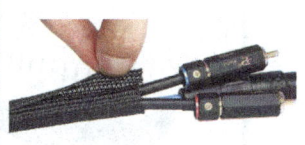

**Cord Protector**

Flexible material covers cords to keep kittens from chewing on them.

$7.99

**Kitten Nail Scissors**

Nail trimming scissors sized for small kittens.

$4.95

**Deluxe Nail Clippers**

Clip cats' and kittens' nails with these heavy duty nail trimmers.

$9.99

**Cat Grooming Hammock**

Hanging bag makes nail trims easy! Zippers and velcro for easy access.

$19.98

**Flea Comb**

Quality fine-tooth comb captures fleas hidden in cats' fur.

$3.99

# KITTEN LOVE  PET STORE CATALOG

**Small Litter Box**

Plastic litter box for small kittens age 8-12 weeks old.

**$6.96**

**Metal Litter Box**

Large, sturdy, stainless steel box is ideal for multiple cat household.

**$38.99**

**Throwaway Litter Boxes**

Replace disposable cat boxes every 2-3 weeks. Pack of 6.

**$21.90**

**Best Cat Litter**

Multi-cat, no scent litter. Kitten-safe formula made with corn. 15 lbs.

**$20.98**

**Metal Litter Scoop**

Waterproof, easy-to-clean litter scoop for cat boxes.

**$6.95**

**Heavy Duty Litter Scoop**

Jumbo size metal litter scoop with soft, easy-grip handle.

**$8.98**

**Litter Genie & Scoop**

Keep litter area clean and fresh. Comes with scoop and 2 bag refills.

**$28.99**

**Kitty Litter Mat**

Large mat keeps litter from sticking to paws. Easy clean design.

**$10.95**

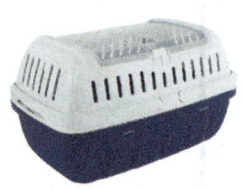

**Sturdy Cat Carrier**

Heavy-duty carrier fits two small or one large cat up to 15 pounds.

**$34.97**

**Cardboard Cat Carrier**

Disposable carrier fits small to medium-sized cat. Pack of 3.

**$27.99**

**Sort Cat Brush**

Real wood handle and soft bristles are gentle on sensitive skin.

**$11.99**

**Self-Cleaning Cat Brush**

Plastic brush with long bristles for grooming cats. Easy to clean.

**$12.90**

**Cat Ball Collection**

Set of 3 toys includes crinkle toy, soccer ball, and jingle ball.

**$5.95**

**Cat Wand Toy**

Wand toy with 7 feather and worm attachments for interactive play.

**$9.96**

**Kitten Breakaway Collar**

Cute cat collar in size small has breakaway safety clasp.

**$6.95**

**Breakaway Cat Collar**

Soft, adjustable collar grows with your kitty. Includes name tag.

**$8.99**

# BUYING KITTEN SUPPLIES

**You have $400 to spend on kitten supplies.** List each item below, then add your total. **Round up** to the nearest dollar ($4.99 —> $5.00) to make adding easier.

HINT: **Always round UP when shopping.** If you round down, the total will seem less than it actually is, and you might not have enough money!

| ITEM | PRICE | QUANTITY | TOTAL |
|---|---|---|---|
| | | | |
| | | | |
| | | | |
| | | | |
| | | | |
| | | | |
| | | | |
| | | | |
| | | | |
| | | | |
| | | | |
| | | | |
| | | | |
| | | | |
| | | | |
| | | | |
| | | | |
| | | | |
| | | | |
| | | | **GRAND TOTAL** |

How much money do you have left over? $_____

# KITTEN PROOF YOUR HOME

Soon, your kittens will be exploring your whole house and making it their own! But before that happens, you have to make your home safe for them.

**Circle the things in the picture that could be dangerous for your kittens.**

**Check the answer key and count how many you guessed correctly.**

Give yourself **ten points** for each one you got right. How did you do? _____ points

**0–40 points:** There are more hidden dangers lurking! See what else you can find.

**50-70 points:** It's getting safer, but there are still some things that can hurt kittens.

**80-100 points:** Great job! You're a pro at making your home safe for kittens!

# KEEPING KITTENS SAFE FROM DANGER

So many things in your house can be dangerous for kittens! But when you know what the dangers are, you can keep your kittens safe.

Let's play a memory game. **Look at the words below for one minute. Then close your eyes & say all the words you remember.**

Give yourself points at the bottom of the page.

| chocolate | string | hot drinks | plants and flowers |
| --- | --- | --- | --- |
| rubber bands | electric cords | onions | plastic bags |
|  | small objects | cleaning sprays | pills and medicine |

**Give yourself 10 points for each one you remembered:** _____ points

Many people have an easier time remembering if they draw or see a picture. **Draw a picture in each box of that item. Then play again and see if you can remember more things.**

**Give yourself 10 points for each one you remembered with pictures:** _____ points

Did you remember more with pictures?    YES    NO

# SHARING KITTEN RESPONSIBILITIES

Taking care of kittens is so much fun, but it's a lot of work! Luckily, you don't have to do it all yourself. You will share kitten jobs and responsibilities with another person.

**Who will you share kitten responsibilities with this week?** _____

**Divide the tasks so each person spends the EXACT SAME AMOUNT OF TIME caring for kittens.**

| Kitten Care Activity | Minutes | Person In Charge |
|---|---|---|
| feed breakfast | 5 | |
| play with kittens: morning | 30 | |
| clean litter boxes | 10 | |
| brush kittens | 25 | |
| feed lunch | 5 | |
| clip claws | 20 | |
| take to vet | 40 | |
| feed dinner | 5 | |
| play with kittens: evening | 25 | |
| hide treats for kittens to find at night | 15 | |

**How much time will each person spend on kitten care next week?** _____ minutes

WORK SPACE

21

# ROUNDING X's GAME

 2-4 players

 game board (page 105), deck of cards

**Get Ready**

- Print* or copy the Rounding X's game board on page 105 for each player.
- Remove the Jacks, Queens, Kings, and Jokers from the deck. Aces = 1
- Put the cards in a pile face down on the table.

**Play**

1. Draw two cards. Make a 2-digit decimal number with the cards.
   (For the decimal point, you can use a die or other small object.)

2. Say the decimal name of the number: "sixty-two hundredths".
   (Don't say, "point six two". Challenge yourself to say the fraction number.)

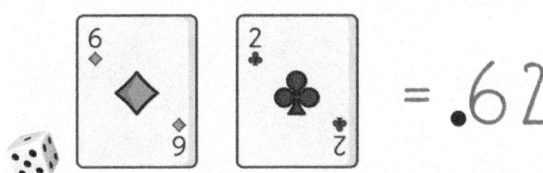

3. Round the number to the nearest tenths place and say the new number out loud: "six tenths".

4. Put an X in the box with the rounded number.

5. The first player to cross off ALL their boxes wins!

| | |
|---|---|
| 0.1 ONE TENTH | 0.2 TWO TENTHS |
| 0.3 THREE TENTHS | 0.4 FOUR TENTHS |
| 0.5 FIVE TENTHS | ✗ SIX TENTHS |
| 0.7 SEVEN TENTHS | 0.8 EIGHT TENTHS |
| 0.9 NINE TENTHS | 1.0 ONE WHOLE |

 *Get printable game boards and videos of how to play at **artfulmath.com/kitten2-goodies**

# GET TO KNOW YOUR KITTENS

What Are Your Kittens' Purr-sonalities?

How Do Your Kittens Like to be Petted?

What Are Your Kittens' Favorite Toys?

Toy Shopping

The "I Love My Kittens" Game

# WHAT ARE YOUR KITTENS' PURR-SONALITIES?

Your kittens are so unique and fun, with their own special quirks and personalities. The more you get to know your little fur babies, the more you love them! 🥰
Let's explore how your kittens are **similar** and **different**.

1. **Write your kittens' names** under the Venn diagram circles on the next page.
2. **Cut apart the Kitten Purr-sonality Words on page 118.**
3. **Sort the words** in the Venn diagram to show each kitten's personality. Then glue them.

### How a Venn Diagram Works

A Venn diagram has two circles that overlap in the middle. Here, we will give each kitten their own circle.

The first circle has words that describe Mr. McFuzz. The words in the second circle describe Sweet Pea.

**Words that describe BOTH kittens go in the middle section, where both circles overlap.**

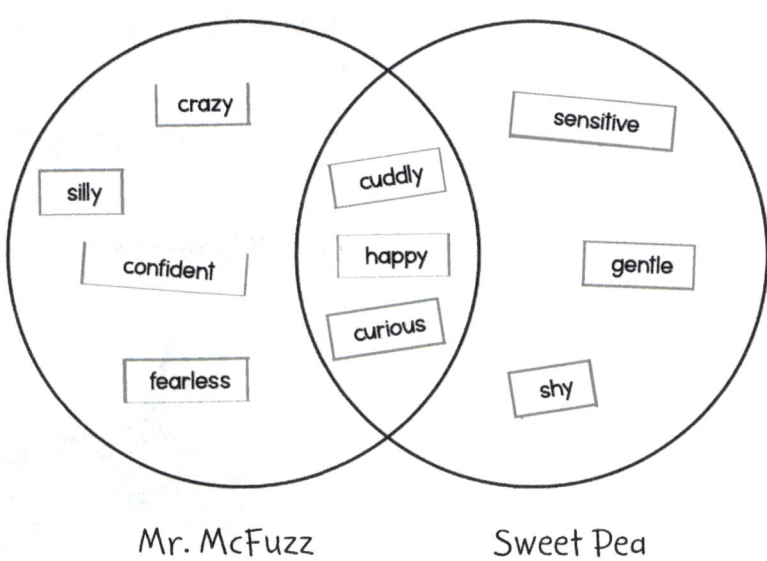

Mr. McFuzz          Sweet Pea

What are two words that describe Mr. McFuzz? _____ and _____

What are two words that describe Sweet Pea? _____ and _____

What are two words that describe BOTH kittens? _____ and _____

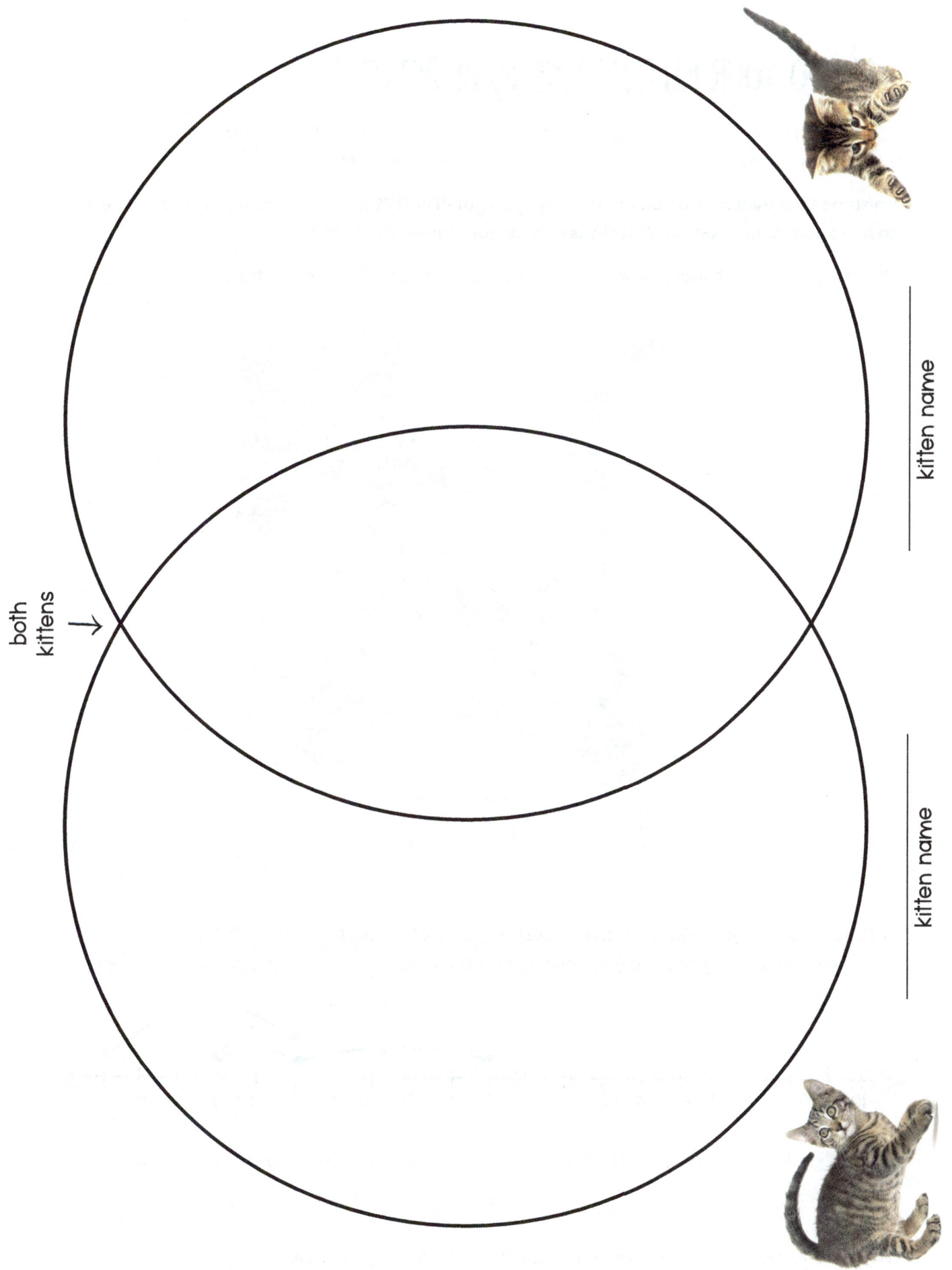

# HOW DO YOUR KITTENS LIKE TO BE PETTED?

As you are petting and cuddling your kittens, you notice that each kitten has certain places where they like to be touched, and other places where they don't.

**Imagine that every time you pet a kitten, you get POSITIVE (plus) points for places they like to be touched, and NEGATIVE (minus) points for places they don't like.**

Here's a picture that shows where many cats do and don't like to be petted.

**Let's say you pet your kitten on their HEAD (+5), BACK (+2), BELLY (−2) and CHIN (+5).**
When you are adding positive (+) and negative (−) numbers, it helps to use a number line.

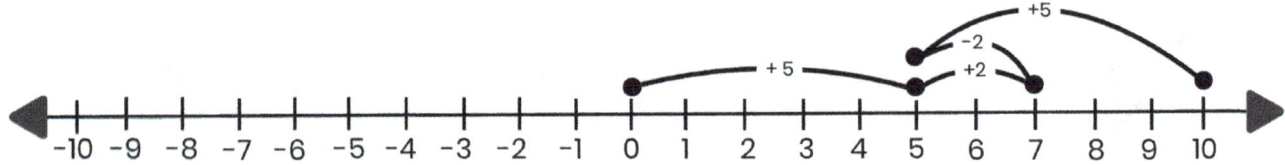

Start at zero. Then jump up 5, back 2, up 2, and up 5 more. Your score is 10..

What would be your score if you pet your kitten's CHIN, TAIL, and HEAD? _____ points

A bunch of kids at a cat café were petting kittens. Some kids obviously knew all about cats, and the cats were happy when they petted them. Other kids didn't really know what they were doing, and pet them in ways the cats didn't like.

**Give these kids a "petting cats score". Start at zero on the number line, then count up and back to figure out each person's score.**

Taylor petted Fluff under the chin and behind one ear.

POINTS: _____

Sam petted Baby on the head, chest, tail, and butt.

POINTS: _____

Sabina petted Tiger behind the ear, under the chin, on his head, and on his back.

POINTS: _____

Mika petted Mochi on the back, on the tummy, and on all four cute feet.

POINTS: _____

Ari petted Scooby on his back, tail, belly, and butt.

POINTS: _____

Ryan petted Archie behind both ears, on his chin, and on his fluffy belly.

POINTS: _____

Keisha petted Miya on the belly, head, and two fluffy paws.

POINTS: _____

Larry petted BooBoo on both back legs, under the chin, and behind both ears.

POINTS: _____

Who was **best** at petting? _____

Who was **worst** at petting? _____

Where would you pet your kittens? _____

What would your score be? _____

# WHAT ARE YOUR KITTENS' FAVORITE TOYS?

Which toys do your kittens like best? Play this game to find out!

**Roll a die and multiply for each kitten, then put a check by the toy or toys that your kittens like best.**

1. **Roll a die** for each kitten. Write the number in the box.

2. Do the **math problem**. **Match the answer** to the toy. This is the toy that kitten likes best!

3. **Check** the toy(s) that you will buy for your kittens.

## Jingle Ball vs Crinkle Ball

Roll a die ↓

Kitten 1  ☐ x 3 = _____

Kitten 2  ☐ x 3 = _____

Match to the answer

| jingle ball | crinkle ball |
|---|---|
|  |  |
| 3-9 | 12-18 |

Check what you want to buy

■ jingle balls
■ crinkle balls

## Springs vs Puff Ball

Kitten 1  ☐ x 5 = _____

Kitten 2  ☐ x 5 = _____

| springs | puff ball |
|---|---|
| 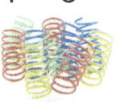 |  |
| 5-15 | 20-30 |

■ springs
■ puff ball

## Fur Mouse vs Felt Mouse

Kitten 1  ☐ x 10 = _____

Kitten 2  ☐ x 10 = _____

| fur mouse | felt mouse |
|---|---|
|  |  |
| 10-30 | 40-60 |

■ fur mouse
■ felt mouse

**Hidey-Hole Mat vs Fish Play Mat**

Kitten 1 ☐ x 4 = _____

Kitten 2 ☐ x 4 = _____

hidey-hole mat    fish play mat

4-12      16-24

▪ hidey-hole mat
▪ fish play mat

**Short Tunnel vs 3-Way Tunnel**

Kitten 1 ☐ x 2 = _____

Kitten 2 ☐ x 2 = _____

short tunnel    3-way tunnel

2-6      8-12

▪ short tunnel
▪ 3-way tunnel

**Ball Toy vs Puzzle Toy**

Kitten 1 ☐ x 6 = _____

Kitten 2 ☐ x 6 = _____

ball toy    puzzle toy

6-18      24-36

▪ ball toy
▪ puzzle toy

**Crinkle Snakes or Chew Sticks**

Kitten 1 ☐ x 9 = _____

Kitten 2 ☐ x 9 = _____

 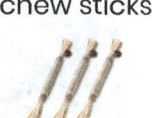

snakes    chew sticks

9-27      36-54

▪ crinkle snakes
▪ chew sticks

Now that you know what your kittens like, you're ready to go shopping! **Look through the catalog on the following pages and put a check by the things you want to buy.**

# KITTEN LOVE  PET STORE CATALOG

**Crinkle Balls**

Twelve lightweight toys with a fun crinkle sound keep kitty entertained.

**$5.99**

**Jingle Bell Balls**

Kittens love these jingly plastic balls with bells inside. Set of 6.

**$6.95**

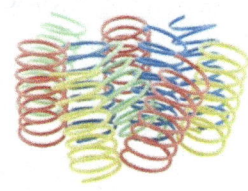

**Spring Toys**

Lightweight springs are bouncy and easy for kittens to carry. 12 set.

**$5.99**

**Rainbow Puff Ball Toy**

Fuzzy, lightweight ball made of puff balls with bell inside.

**$7.99**

**Fur Mouse Cat Toy**

Realistic, furry mouse toy has real deer fur and leather tail.

**$6.95**

**Felt Mouse Toy**

Adorable, fuzzy mouse toy made of real wool.

**$4.99**

**Squeaky Mouse Set**

These furry mice make a squeaking sound when touched. Set of 2.

**$7.99**

**Fuzzy Tunnel**

Extra-long cat tunnel with fur includes peep holes and hanging toy.

**$19.98**

**Lightweight Cat Tunnel**

See-through tunnel sized for kittens. Includes hanging toys.

**$8.95**

**Three-way Cat Tunnel**

Hide, pounce, and play with three entrances and peep hole on top.

**$11.96**

**Ball Track Toy**

Interactive ball toy with three levels. Multi-cat or solo play.

**$8.97**

**Cat Puzzle Toy**

Fun toy and maze game with ball inside keeps cats active & engaged.

**$16.99**

**Play Mat Rug with Holes**

Filled with waves and holes for kitty to hide, pounce, and play.

**$35.95**

**Underwater Play Mat**

Floating plastic fish inside a water-filled mat keep kitty entertained.

**$19.99**

**Silvervine Chew Sticks**

Naturally-scented chew sticks keep your cat's teeth healthy.

**$6.99**

**Catnip Crinkle Snakes**

Irresistible catnip scent and crinkle sound give cats hours of fun.

**$9.98**

# KITTEN LOVE ♥ PET STORE CATALOG

**Wand Toy and Refills**

Sturdy wand with extra feathers and worm toy for interactive play.

$7.99

**Fun Fish Kicker Toys**

Set of two large fish with crinkle sound for kicking and wrestling.

$12.95

**Donut Bed Scratcher**

Comfy bed, tunnel, and scratcher all in one! Made of sturdy felt.

$39.95

**Cat Chew Stick Ropes**

Three catnip ropes for chewing, teeth cleaning, and safe biting.

$7.99

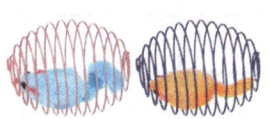

**Springy Mouse Toy (2)**

Stretchable, lightweight, springy plastic balls with furry mice inside.

$6.95

**Furry Kicker Toy**

Catnip-scented, fuzzy kicker toys with crinkle sound. Set of 3.

$9.98

**Catnip Banana**

Sturdy canvas kicker toys are filled with the best quality catnip.

$15.99

**Springy Tube Cat Toys**

Mesh tubes are the perfect size for kittens to carry around. 4 set.

$3.95

**Interactive Play Mat**

Crinkly mat with three electronic toys that shake and move.

$23.99

**Interactive Rope Toy**

Moving cat ball with elastic mesh tail. Charger included.

$20.99

**Kitten Plushie Set**

16 adorable, tiny plush toys for cats and kittens.

$13.97

**Rainbow Worm toys**

Four google-eyed worms with soft bodies and feathers.

$6.99

**Deluxe Toy Set**

30 balls, springs, bells, and other fun cat toys to chase and play.

$19.99

**Cat Crazies Chaser Toys**

Lightweight toys with a shape that's perfect for chasing and carrying.

$2.99

**Catnip Cats**

Colorful companions and kicker toys. Include 5 scented stuffies.

$6.99

**Flapping Bird**

Fluffy, feathered bird toy has flapping wings and a realistic chirp.

$8.98

# GOING TOY SHOPPING

Great news: all toys in the pet store are on sale for **50% off** (half off), today!
**You have $150 to spend on toys.** List each item below, then add up your total.

| ITEM | REGULAR PRICE | SALE PRICE | QUANTITY | TOTAL |
|---|---|---|---|---|
|  |  |  |  |  |
|  |  |  |  |  |
|  |  |  |  |  |
|  |  |  |  |  |
|  |  |  |  |  |
|  |  |  |  |  |
|  |  |  |  |  |
|  |  |  |  |  |
|  |  |  |  |  |
|  |  |  |  |  |
|  |  |  |  |  |
|  |  |  |  |  |
|  |  |  |  |  |
|  |  |  |  |  |
|  |  |  |  |  |
|  |  |  |  |  |
|  |  |  |  | GRAND TOTAL |

HINT: Round up, then cut that price in half.   $7.99 —> $8.00
Half of $8.00 is $4.00.

Half of $3.00 is $1.50.
Half of $5.00 is $2.50.
What pattern do you notice when dividing odd numbers in half?

# THE "I LOVE MY KITTENS" GAME

1. **Roll a die** to fill in the spaces below.
2. **Do the math** with your numbers to answer each kitten question.

**How many furry, purry kisses will you give your kittens in a half hour?**

___ + ___ + ___ + ___ + ___ = ☐

**How many stinky poops can two kittens make in a week?**

___ + ___ + ___ + ___ + ___ = ☐

**How many toys will your kittens destroy in one week?**

___ x ___ = ☐

**How many stories about your adorable kittens will you tell your friends next time you see them?**

___ ___ + ___ ___ = ☐

**Write your own question:**

_____?

___ ___ + ___ ___ + ___ ___ = ☐

# NUMBER HOP GAME

 2 players

 number line (page 106), deck of cards

**Get Ready**
- Remove any Jacks, Queens, Kings, and Jokers from the deck.
- Put the pile of cards face down in front of you.

**Play**

1. Each person takes two cards from the deck and turns them over.

2 BLACK cards are positive numbers. RED cards are negative numbers. Add the two cards together.

   + 3 and -9 = -6

3. Use the number line on page 106 to help you. Start at zero, then **count up for positive numbers** and **back for negative numbers**.

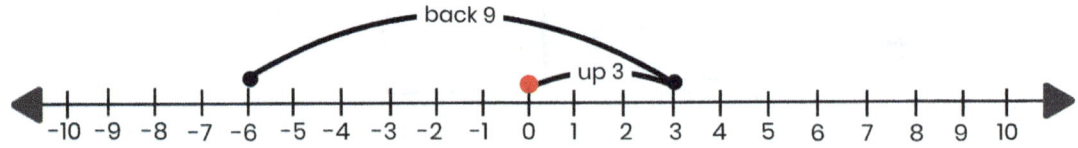

4. The person with the higher total takes all four cards. Set these cards aside—each card equals one point.

5. Play until all your cards are gone. The player with the most points wins!

*LEVEL UP! Draw three cards on each turn.*

 *Get printable game boards and videos of how to play at **artfulmath.com/kitten2-goodies***

# HUNGRY KITTENS

How Much Do Your Kittens Eat?

Be a Kitten Food Detective

How Much Meat Do These Foods Have?

The "First 5 Ingredients" Trick

Which Foods Get the Highest Score?

Buying Kitten Food

# HOW MUCH DO YOUR KITTENS EAT?

It's time to feed your kittens!
Did you know a 6-month-old kitten eats MORE than a full-grown cat?!
ONE kitten eats at least 6 ounces of wet food per day.

**TWO kittens eat at least _____ ounces of wet food per day.**

**How many 3-ounce cans of food do you need per day to feed your 2 kittens?** _____ cans per day

**How many cans of kitten food will you need for ONE WEEK?**
_____ cans per week

**How many cans of kitten food will you need for ONE MONTH?**
_____ cans per month (30 days)

You have 10 cans of kitten food in the house.

**How long will that last you?** _____ days

**If today is a Thursday, what day of the week will you have to buy kitten food?** _____

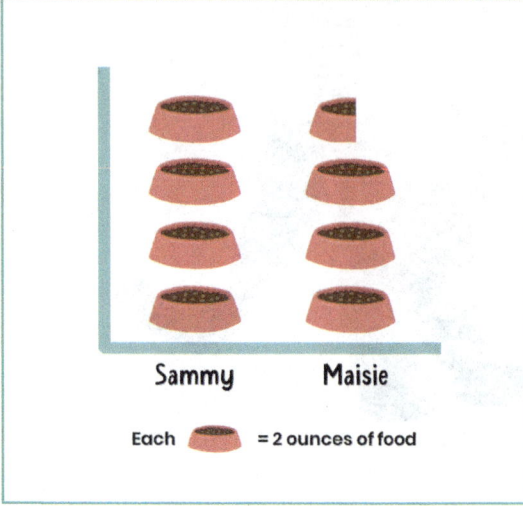

Each 🥣 = 2 ounces of food

Kittens Sammy and Maisie were extra hungry. The pictogram shows what they ate yesterday.

Can you figure out how much they ate?

**Sammy ate** _____ **ounces of food**

**Maisie ate** _____ **ounces of food**

# BE A KITTEN FOOD DETECTIVE

**How do you know which is the best food for your kittens?**
To find out, you'll need to become a cat food detective!

Cats are **carnivores,** meaning almost all their food should be meat.
Some cat food makers use cheap ingredients and grains that are less healthy for cats.

There are rules about what people can name their cat food.
**The words in the name give clues to how much meat is inside.** That way, pet parents like you can tell just by reading the name if it's a healthy food or an unhealthy food.

## If you see words like "chicken cat food" or "beef for cats", that means it's at least 95% meat

If you see the words like "chicken cat food", that means it's almost all meat inside—95%! (You will almost never see this, since store-bought cat food has many different ingredients.)

"PERCENT" MEANS "OUT OF 100". IF A CAN OF FOOD WAS MADE OF 100 BITS, 95 WOULD BE MEAT.

## If it says "dinner", "recipe", "entree", "formula" or "feast", it has at least 25% meat

You might see cat food called Chicken Dinner, Fish Recipe, Beef Formula, and so on. These words tell you that **at least 25% of the ingredients are meat** (between 25% and 95%).

COLOR IN 25 BOXES TO SHOW THE **MINIMUM AMOUNT** OF MEAT IN EACH CAN OF FOOD

## If you see the word "with" in the title (such as "with chicken"), it has at least 3% meat

If you see the word "with" in the name, that means it has **at least 3 percent meat** (between 3% and 25%.) They are trying to trick you into thinking the food has a lot of meat, when it doesn't.

COLOR IN 3 BOXES TO SHOW THE **MINIMUM AMOUNT** OF MEAT IN EACH CAN OF FOOD

## If you see the word "flavor" in the name, that means it has LESS than 3% meat!

The word "flavor" just means "taste". If a bag or can says "flavor", there is **almost no actual meat**! Don't be fooled by fancy packaging. Look for clues to what's really inside.

COLOR IN 1 OR 2 BOXES TO SHOW WHAT LESS THAN 3% LOOKS LIKE

# HOW MUCH MEAT DO THESE FOODS HAVE?

The CLUE WORDS on the labels of kitten food will tell you how much meat is inside. Makers of cat food are required by law to use certain words that tell you what **percent of meat** it has:

— The words **RECIPE, FEAST, DINNER, ENTRÉE, FORMULA** mean it has AT LEAST 25% MEAT
— The word **WITH** means it has AT LEAST 3% MEAT
— The word **FLAVOR** means it has LESS THAN 3% MEAT

**Read the labels below and look for the clue words. Then write how much meat each food has.**

1.

CLUE WORD: _____

HAS AT LEAST _____ % MEAT

2.

CLUE WORD: _____

HAS AT LEAST _____ % MEAT

3.

CLUE WORD: _____

HAS AT LEAST _____ % MEAT

4.

CLUE WORD: _____

HAS AT LEAST _____ % MEAT

5.

CLUE WORD: _____

HAS AT LEAST _____ % MEAT

6.

CLUE WORD: _____

HAS AT LEAST _____ % MEAT

# THE "FIRST 5 INGREDIENTS" TRICK

You've watched for clues on the label, and picked out some foods that look healthy. Still, some foods are better than others. To find the very best kitten foods, **look on the back of the can at the ingredients list. You only need to read the first five ingredients.**

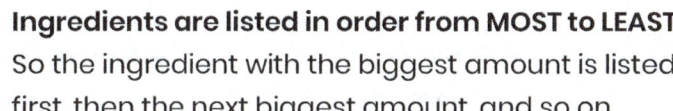

**Ingredients are listed in order from MOST to LEAST.** So the ingredient with the biggest amount is listed first, then the next biggest amount, and so on.

**Which ingredient is there MOST of in this food?**

_____

**Does the label above look like it would be a healthy food for your kittens?**

YES        NO

Why? _____

_____

 Kittens and cats need lots of **protein** (meat, fish, and eggs). A good cat food will have lots of protein in the first 5 ingredients.

 Grains (like wheat, soy, or rice) do NOT have protein. You might see grains in foods that are **not as healthy** for cats and kittens.

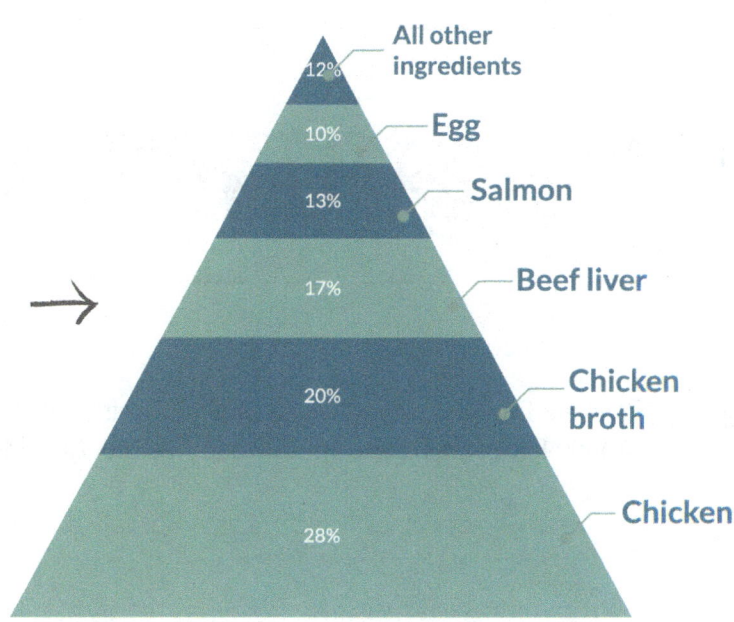

This pyramid chart shows the ingredients from the cat food label above.

There is 28% chicken in this kitten food.

**What might be the name of this food?**

A. Chicken Flavor Kitten Chow
B. Kitten Food with Chicken
C. Chicken Dinner for Kittens

**After chicken, which ingredient is there most of?**

_____

**Which ingredient has HALF the amount of chicken broth?**

_____

# WHICH FOODS GET THE HIGHEST SCORE?

You are at the pet store, trying to pick out the very best food for your kittens. You decide to **give each food a score** so you can compare them.

**SCORE CARD**

| Chicken, beef, fish, liver, broth, lamb, salmon, egg | Meat by-products, flavors, oil, fat, water, milk, vegetables, tallow | Corn, wheat gluten, soybeans, rice |
|---|---|---|
| **PLUS 2 POINTS** | **0 POINTS** | **MINUS 2 POINTS** |

Look at the FIRST 5 INGREDIENTS in the food labels below. Add the points for each one.

**#1 WET**
Chicken, liver, fish, meat by-products, water, artificial and natural flavors, rice, MINERALS [potassium chloride, magnesium proteinate, zinc sulfate, ferrous

____ ____ ____ ____ ____ = Score: ____

**#2 WET**
Lamb, Water Sufficient for Processing, Lamb Tripe, Lamb Heart, Lamb Kidney, Lamb Spleen, Lamb Liver, Lamb Blood, Ground Lamb Bone, New

____ ____ ____ ____ ____ = Score: ____

**#3 DRY**
INGREDIENTS: Whole Ground Corn, Chicken By-Product Meal, Corn Protein Meal, Soybean Meal, Animal Fat (Preserved With Mixed Tocopherols), Whole Wheat,

____ ____ ____ ____ ____ = Score: ____

**#4 WET**
Chicken, Chicken Liver, Chicken Broth, Carrots, Natural Flavor, Cranberries, Guar Gum, Ground Flaxseed, Potassium Chloride, Taurine, Salt, Menhaden Fish Oil (preserved with

____ ____ ____ ____ ____ = Score: ____

**#5 WET**
INGREDIENTS: FISH BROTH, FISH, CHICKEN, SALMON, WHEAT GLUTEN, OCEAN FISH, MODIFIED TAPIOCA STARCH, POULTRY BY-PRODUCTS, TUNA, SUGAR, CHICKEN

____ ____ ____ ____ ____ = Score: ____

**#6**
DRY

**INGREDIENTS** Chicken by-product meal, corn protein meal, rice, soy flour, animal fat preserved with mixed-tocopherols,

_____  _____  _____  _____  _____  = Score: _____

---

**#7**
DRY

**ingredients** Water, chicken, wheat gluten, meat by-products, liver, rice, powder spinach, artificial and natural flavors, soy flour, tricalcium phosphate, **MINERALS**

_____  _____  _____  _____  _____  = Score: _____

---

**#8**
WET

Chicken, meat by-products, liver, chicken broth, fish, milk, egg product, artificial and natural flavors, **MINERALS** [potassium chloride, magnesium proteinate, zinc sulfate, ferrous

_____  _____  _____  _____  _____  = Score: _____

---

**#9**
DRY

**INGREDIENTS:** GROUND CORN, CHICKEN BY-PRODUCT MEAL, SOYBEAN MEAL, CORN PROTEIN MEAL, BEEF TALLOW (MIXED TOCOPHEROLS USED AS A PRESERVATIVE),

_____  _____  _____  _____  _____  = Score: _____

---

**#10**
WET

Chicken, Chicken Liver, Chicken Broth, Vegetable Broth, Salmon Oil (Preserved With Mixed Tocopherols), Natural Flavor, Dried Egg Product,

_____  _____  _____  _____  _____  = Score: _____

---

**Write the scores:**

#1 ____     #2 ____     #3 ____     #4 ____     #5 ____     #6 ____     #7 ____     #8 ____     #9 ____     #10 ____
wet         wet         dry         wet         wet         dry         dry         wet         dry         wet

**Which three foods were THE BEST?** _____ _____ _____

**Which three foods were THE WORST?** _____ _____ _____

**Look at your ratings for wet food vs dry food. What do you notice?** _____
_____

**Would you rather buy dry food or wet food for your kittens?**     DRY     WET

**Why?** _____

# BUYING KITTEN FOOD

It's time to figure out how much food to buy and what it will cost.

Two kittens eat 4 cans of food per day.
**How many cans of food will you need for one month (30 days)?** _____ cans

Kitten food is .99 cents each. **How much will it cost to buy 30 days worth of food?**
(HINT: Round up!)   $_____

Good news! Your local pet store has a sale on food: **Buy 3, get one free!**

| $1 | $1 | $1 | ⊠ |

**Buy 3, Get One FREE**
Get 4 cans of .99 cent food for just $3.00.

If you arranged all your food up in groups of four, each group would cost just $3 (not $4).

$3    $6    $9    $12    $15

Since it would take a long time to count like that, here's another way to think about it.
**You are paying for 3 out of 4 cans. So you are paying for just 3/4 cans.**

3/4
| $30 | $30 | $30 | $30 |
———— $120 ————

Find the regular price, then figure out 3/4 of that.

3/4 of 120 = _____

**How much money did you save using the discount?** $_____

You brought $100 to the store. **How much money will you have left over?** $_____

**What would the price be if you bought 20 cans?** $_____
**How much would you save?** $_____

———— $20 ————

**What would the price be if you bought 44 cans?** $_____
**How much would you save?** $_____

———— $44 ————

**1. You walk into a pet store and see a small can of kitten food.**
It says it has 3 ounces of meat inside.

Is that a lot? Is it a little? You don't know!
"It doesn't sound like very much," you say.

Then you see a larger can of kitten food. It also has 3 ounces of meat.
**Both the large can and the small can have the same amount of meat.**

**Which cat food has more meat per ounce?**   SMALL CAN   LARGE CAN

---

**2. You find a new cat food online: Kitty Baby cat food has forty 5-star reviews!**

Does this mean it's a great food? Well, that depends....

**There are a total of 1,000 reviews for that cat food. Only 40 out of 1,000 reviews have 5 stars.**

40/1000 is 4/100, or 4%.   Shade in 4%.

**A different food, Kitten Yum, also has 40 5-star reviews, but it has just 50 reviews altogether.**

40/50 is 80%.   Shade in 80%.

**Which is the better food?**   KITTY BABY   KITTEN YUM

---

**3. A bag of cat food says it has "one pound of meat".**
That sounds like a lot. But then you see it's a 20-pound bag of food.

1/20 is 5%.   Shade in 5%.

**A different food also has one pound of meat. This one is a 5-pound bag.**

1/5 is 20%.   Shade in 20%.

**Which bag of food has more meat per pound?**   20-pound bag   5-pound bag

---

**How can percentages help you?** _____

_____

# FRACTION CATS GAME

 2 players

 game board (page 107), dice, markers, beans

## Get Ready

- Print* or copy the game board on page 107. Give each player a colored marker.
- Put 24 beans on the table.

## Play

1. Roll one die. If you get a 5, roll again.

2. Find a cat fraction on the game board that includes the number you rolled. Color it in. (If you roll a three, you could color in 1/3, 2/3, 3/4, or 3/6.)

   I colored in 2/3 since it has a 3 in it.

3. Find that fraction of 24. You can use the beans to help you. (See example below.)

4. If you roll a number that is no longer on the board, skip your turn.

5. When all the cat fractions are colored, count your points. The player with the highest score wins!

---

**EXAMPLE: Find 2/3 of 24**

— Since the fraction is THIRDS, divide the beans equally into THREE groups

— Your fraction is **two** thirds, so count the number of beans in TWO groups. (16)
— Your score for the round is 16.

---

LEVEL UP! Play with 36 beans. Or, for an easier game, play with 12 beans.

 *Get printable game boards and videos of how to play at **artfulmath.com/kitten2-goodies**

# LIFE WITH KITTENS

What Do Your Kittens Do All Day?

Which Kitten is More Playful?

How High Can Kittens Jump?

Make a Kitten Toy Schedule

What Do Your Kittens Need?

Why Do Kittens Get in Trouble?

# WHAT DO YOUR KITTENS DO ALL DAY?

What's a typical day in the life of a kitten? How much time do they spend on each activity? You decide to keep track of what your kittens do all day.

**Write how many hours your kittens spend on each activity in one day.
The total must add up to 24 hours.**

| Sleep | Play | Zoomies | Go Potty | Groom | Look out window | |
|---|---|---|---|---|---|---|
| ☐ + | ☐ + | ☐ + | ☐ + | ☐ + | ☐ | = 24 |
| hours | hours | hours | hours | hours | hours | hours |

**Color in the boxes below to show how much time kittens spent doing each activity.**
Use a different color for each activity. Each square represents one hour.

☐☐☐☐☐☐☐☐☐☐☐☐☐☐☐☐☐☐☐☐☐☐☐☐ = 1 day

**What fraction of the day did your kittens spend playing?** _____ / 24
Is there a simpler way to write that fraction? (Example: 12/24 = 6/12 = 1/2) _____

**What fraction of the day did your kittens spend sleeping?** _____
Some people say that cats spend 1/3 of their day sleeping. Do you agree?   YES   NO

**What fraction of the day did your kittens spend grooming (cleaning themselves)?** _____

**Which TWO activities did your kittens spend the most time doing?**
_____ and _____   How many hours altogether? _____

**What fraction of the day did your kittens SLEEP and GROOM themselves?** _____

**What fraction of the day did your kittens PLAY and have ZOOMIES?** _____

**Draw a tiny picture of a kitten with the zoomies:**

# WHICH KITTEN IS MORE PLAYFUL?

Both of your kittens love to play, but is one more playful than the other? A kitty-cam reveals your kittens' play behaviors for the past 24 hours.

**Read the data for both your kittens, then answer the questions below.**

**Kitten 1 name** _____

**Kitten 2 name** _____

**PLAY TIMES**
- 5:45am to 6:20am played with bug
- 1:15pm to 1:35pm in the bathtub, loudly
- 5:20pm to 6:10pm in cardboard box
- 8:55pm to 9:30pm zoomies
- 1:40am to 2:05am played on your bed

**PLAY TIMES**
- 8:15am to 8:50am in living room
- 11:55am to 12:10pm in a paper bag
- 4:15pm to 4:40pm in the cat tree
- 7:00pm to 7:45pm in toy box
- 9:50pm to 10:20pm zoomies

**How much time did a kitten play in a paper bag?** _____

**How long did a kitten play in a cardboard box?** _____

**Which kitten spent the most time acting crazy with the zoomies?** _____

**Which kitten woke you up in the middle of the night?** _____

**How many minutes did Kitten 1 play?** _____

**Convert Kitten 1's play time into hours and minutes:** _____ hours _____ minutes

**How many minutes did Kitten 2 play?** _____

**Convert Kitten 2's play time into hours and minutes:** _____ hours _____ minutes

**Which kitten played more?** _____ **How much more?** _____ minutes

# HOW HIGH CAN KITTENS JUMP?

Your kittens are always jumping on things! They're really good at it.
**Kittens can jump 5 times their height! How high can these kittens jump?**

*We kittens can jump FIVE TIMES our height!*

**1**
9 inches tall
can jump
_____ inches

**2**
5 inches tall
can jump
_____ inches

**3**
10 inches tall
can jump
_____ inches

**4**
6 inches tall
can jump
_____ inches

**5**
7 inches tall
can jump
_____ inches

**6**
13 inches tall
can jump
_____ inches

**7**
8 inches tall
can jump
_____ inches

**8**
12 inches tall
can jump
_____ inches

**9**
14 inches tall
can jump
_____ inches

**10**
11 inches tall
can jump
_____ inches

**Convert these kittens' jumping heights to feet and inches.**

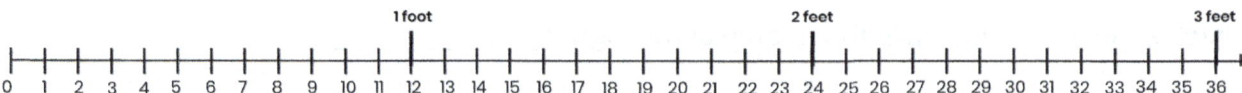

Divide each kitten's jumping height in inches by 12.

$$12\overline{)30}\phantom{0} \begin{array}{c} 2\,\text{R6} \end{array}$$

An answer of "2 remainder 6" is 2 feet 6 inches.

KITTEN 1: _____ feet _____ inches

KITTEN 2: _____ feet _____ inches

KITTEN 3: _____ feet _____ inches

KITTEN 4: _____ feet _____ inches

KITTEN 5: _____ feet _____ inches

KITTEN 6: _____ feet _____ inches

KITTEN 7: _____ feet _____ inches

KITTEN 8: _____ feet _____ inches

KITTEN 9: _____ feet _____ inches

KITTEN 10: _____ feet _____ inches

# MAKE A KITTEN TOY SCHEDULE

Kittens get bored when they see the same toys every day. Put some of their toys away and bring out just a few each week. Kittens will think they're getting brand new toys!

**Make a schedule so your kittens can play with different toys each week.**

| YOU HAVE THESE TOYS | |
|---|---|
| mouse | spring |
| jingle ball | puzzle toy |
| tunnel | play mat |
| wand toy | kicker toy |
| crinkle toy | puff ball |

**TOY SCHEDULE CHECKLIST**

- Your kittens get **4 different toys** each week.
- The toy **combo is different** each week.
- **Do not** use the same toy **2 weeks in a row**.
- **Each toy is used twice** in the 5-week schedule.

**Cut out the toy words on page 114 and move them around until you find a solution that works.**

This kind of puzzle works best using **trial and error**—testing out lots of different possibilities.

| week 1 | week 2 | week 3 | week 4 | week 5 |
|---|---|---|---|---|
| 1. | 1. | 1. | 1. | 1. |
| 2. | 2. | 2. | 2. | 2. |
| 3. | 3. | 3. | 3. | 3. |
| 4. | 4. | 4. | 4. | 4. |

# WHAT DO YOUR KITTENS NEED?

Kittens who get what they need are healthy, happy, and well behaved! Here is a list of words showing some of the things your kittens need.

**Find the hidden words. Then use those words to finish the sentences below.**

```
S P A L T Y M O Z C R
W L N S I A R X U C P
O P L A Y T I M E H M
B A W H R Q T I K A O
L D C A T T R E E S U
A N T S N O W E R E Y
N R K E V D A Q S R N
K G Z P E N T L Y T X
E D L A Q R E O K O A
T I S K O P R W Y Y I
S C R A T C H E R S D
```

water
litter
scratchers
playtime
cat trees
wand toys
blankets
chaser toys

*Use these words to complete the sentences below!*

1. Cats need wet food because they get most of their _____ from food.

2. _____ are important for cats to sharpen claws, stretch, and relieve stress.

3. Cats need plenty of large, clean _____ boxes.

4. _____ give kittens places to jump, climb, and play.

5. Cat beds and _____ give kittens a cozy place to sleep.

6. _____ with kittens helps them practice hunting, bond with you, and have fun.

7. Different kinds of toys, like _____ and _____, keep kittens' bodies and minds healthy.

# WHY DO KITTENS GET INTO TROUBLE?

Kittens are not trying to be bad when they get into mischief or do things they shouldn't. They are telling you, "There's something I need! Please help me!" Their behavior is a clue to what they need.

**Match the kittens' behavior to what they are thinking (the math problem & answer also match). Then write what each kitten needs in order to stop the bad behavior.**

scratches furniture — 25

goes potty on the floor — 4

chews on dangerous objects — 42

steals food from the table — 55

knocks things off shelves — 64

11 × 5 — "I'm hungry!"   NEEDS healthy food or snacks

36 ÷ 9 — "My litter box is too small for me... and it's dirty!"   NEEDS _____

8 × 8 — "I want to jump, climb, and play in high spaces."   NEEDS _____

100 ÷ 4 — "I need to stretch and keep my claws healthy."   NEEDS _____

6 × 7 — "I get bored seeing the same toys all the time."   NEEDS _____

52

# FEET AND INCHES BUMP GAME

 2 players

 game board and playing pieces (page 116), 2 dice

**Get Ready**

- Print* or copy a game board from page 116.
- Cut out the playing pieces at the bottom of page 116.
- Give each player 6 game pieces. Each player gets a different cat picture.

**Play**

1. Roll 2 dice.

2. Read the number of inches next to the number you rolled.

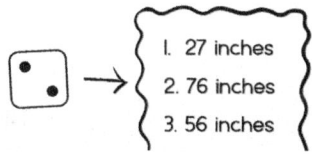

3. Divide the number of inches by 12 to convert it into FEET and INCHES.
   Example: **76 ÷ 12 = 6 R4**, or 6 feet 4 inches.

4. Find the cat with your answer in feet and inches. Put your playing piece on that space.

5. If you get an answer that already has another player's piece on it, **bump them off** and put your piece there instead!

6. The first player to get their 6 playing pieces on the board wins.

 *Get printable game boards and videos of how to play at <u>artfulmath.com/kitten2-goodies</u>

# DESIGN THE PURR-FECT HOME FOR KITTENS

**Design a Kitten-Friendly Home**

**Buying Cat Furniture**

# DESIGN A KITTEN-FRIENDLY HOME

Your kittens are an important part of your family. That means your house should have furniture for both humans and cats! Cats need special furniture for sleeping, scratching, climbing, and play.

**Cut out and paste pictures of furniture to design the ideal home for your kittens. Later, you'll go shopping for the kitten furniture you will add to your home.**

Cut out the furniture pictures on **pages 120–124**.

Use the pictures to design each room in your house.

When you are happy with your plan, glue your pictures in place.

**Here are some kitten facts to keep in mind as you design your cat-friendly home:**

Get scratchers in different shapes and sizes, made of different materials. Put them near sofas and chairs so kittens don't scratch your furniture.

You will need at least one litter box per cat, plus one more. If you have a larger house, you may need more litter boxes.

Try to have a large cat tree in any room kittens spend a lot of time in. The more things your cats have to climb on, the better!

Your living room and bedroom are two of the most important rooms in your house. **Cut out the pictures on pages 120-124 (or print them at artfulmath.com/kitten2-goodies).**

**Arrange the furniture so that each room is a happy place for both cats and humans, then glue the pictures in place.**

## Living Room

Put a check by the cat furniture you want in this room.

- ☐ Cat tree
- ☐ Scratching post
- ☐ Litter box
- ☐ Tunnel or play mat
- ☐ Cat bed or hammock
- ☐ Other:_____

## Your Bedroom

- ☐ Cat tree
- ☐ Scratching post
- ☐ Litter box
- ☐ Tunnel or play mat
- ☐ Cat bed or hammock
- ☐ Other:_____

What other rooms are in your house?

**Write the names** of each room and design them using the pictures on pages 120-124.

**Color and decorate your pictures when you're done.**

_____

Put a check by the cat furniture you want in this room.

◻ Cat tree

◻ Scratching post

◻ Litter box

◻ Tunnel or play mat

◻ Cat bed or hammock

◻ Other:_____

_____

◻ Cat tree

◻ Scratching post

◻ Litter box

◻ Tunnel or play mat

◻ Cat bed or hammock

◻ Other:_____

After you've designed all your rooms, **look through the catalog** on the following pages.

**In the catalog, put a check by the cat furniture you want to buy.**

*Look in the CAT-alog on the next pages. Put a check by the things you want to buy.*

_____

▪ Cat tree

▪ Scratching post

▪ Litter box

▪ Tunnel or play mat

▪ Cat bed or hammock

▪ Other:_____

_____

▪ Cat tree

▪ Scratching post

▪ Litter box

▪ Tunnel or play mat

▪ Cat bed or hammock

▪ Other:_____

**Put a check by cat furniture you would like to buy:**

**Small Cat Tree**
Just the right size for a stretch, some play time, and a nap.
$39.99

**Fluffy Cat Cloud Bed**
Send your kitty off to dreamland with this unbelievably soft bed.
$19.99

**Deluxe Cat Tree**
Extra large tree with 2 cubbies, 3 hammocks, and 3 shelves. Amazing!
$79.00

**Tall Scratching Post**
39" tall scratch post lets cats stretch, climb, and keep claws healthy.
$21.99

**Kitty Cave Bed**
Plush, comfy bed is machine washable and cozy for cats & kittens.
$19.95

**Scratch Post Cave**
It's a kitty cave, shelf, and cat scratcher in one! Scratcher is 24".
$27.99

**Tall Cat Tree Playhouse**
Extra tall cat playground with ramp, covered bed, hammock, and shelves.
$82.99

**Stylish Cat Tree**
The beautiful basket has a deliciously soft, fluffy pillow inside.
$75.99

**Cat Hammock Scratcher**
Soft, furry hammock and double scratcher is comfy and snuggly.
$24.00

**Donut Bed**
Part kitty bed, part tunnel. Encourages cats to scratch and play.
$59.99

**Hanging Cat Hammock**
Soft, fuzzy fabric keeps kitty comfy and warm. Ideal for house or catio.
$19.95

**Large Cat Tree**
A furry cat tree with a tiny ladder, cozy cave, and comfy hammock.
$69.99

**Wall Hammock**
Real wood frame and cotton hammock create a perfect napping spot.
$28.95

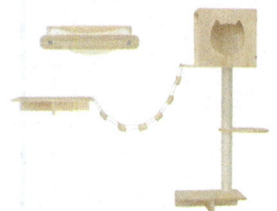
**Cat Wall Furniture Set**
Turn your wall into a cat playground! Scratcher, bridge, and hammock.
$63.99

**Climbing Pole**
A tall, rope-covered pole for kitty to climb and play on indoors.
$65.99

**Wall Shelves**
Rope-covered steps lead kitty up the wall to a cat playground.
$26.00

**Cute Cat Bed**
Adorable kitty bed with fluffy pillow, cat ears, and a sweet little tail.
$24.99

**Jungle Cat Scratcher**
Palm tree scratching posts make kitty feel like a wild thing.
$39.99

**Soft, Cozy Cat Bed**
Large, soft bed is big enough for a large cat or two kittens to share.
$19.95

**Giant Scratching Post**
45" tall and 12" across, this deluxe scratch post is a cat's dream.
$99.99

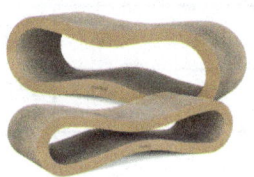
**Double Scratcher Set**
Uniquely-shaped, sturdy cardboard scratchers for double the fun.
$24.98

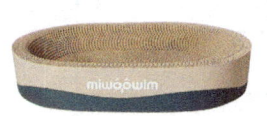
**Scratcher Bed**
Part scratcher, part cat bed. Made from sturdy corrugated cardboard.
$9.95

**Incline Scratcher**
Ramp scratcher with natural rug material for a satisfying stretch.
$24.95

**Mini Kitty Couch**
Adorable, comfy sofa is the perfect size for sleepy cats and kittens.
$39.99

**Cat Floor Hammock**
Comfortable, elevated hammock is portable and easy to clean.
$25.00

**Cat Window Hammock**
Attaches to window so kitty can look out and watch the world.
$27.99

**Floor to Ceiling Cat Tree**
Give cats lots of room to climb with this sturdy, fun cat tree.
$95.00

**Scratcher Carpet**
Can be used on the floor or stuck to a wall for cats to scratch.
$23.95

**Three-Sided Scratcher**
Unique triangle design with recycled cardboard for three times the fun!
$42.95

**Cat Ears Wall Scratcher**
Bamboo and sisal wall scratcher keeps cats happy and healthy.
$26.99

**Hammock Scratcher**
Furry shelves, cave, and two hammocks for hours of play.
$38.99

**Cardboard Cat Castle**
Three levels of shelves and peep holes make cats feel like royalty!
$76.00

# BUYING CAT FURNITURE

You are SO EXCITED to buy scratchers, cat trees, hammocks, and other fun cat furniture. **There's just one tiny problem… you don't have enough money to buy it all at once.**

These things are expensive, so you'll have to get a little at a time.
**You have $120 per month** to spend on cat furniture. Plan what to buy in the coming months.

**MONTH 1:** Total to spend: $120

| ITEM | PRICE |
|---|---|
|  |  |
|  |  |
|  |  |
|  |  |
|  |  |
|  |  |
| **TOTAL** |  |

How much money do you have left over from Month 1?  $_____

**MONTH 2:** Left over from last month  $_____ + $120 = $_____

| ITEM | PRICE |
|---|---|
|  |  |
|  |  |
|  |  |
|  |  |
|  |  |
|  |  |
| **TOTAL** |  |

How much money do you have left over from Month 2?  $_____

**MONTH 3:** Left over from last month  $ _____    + $120  =  $ _____

| ITEM | PRICE |
|---|---|
|  |  |
|  |  |
|  |  |
|  |  |
|  |  |
|  |  |
| TOTAL |  |

How much money do you have left over from Month 3?  $_____


**MONTH 4:** Left over from last month  $ _____    + $120  =  $ _____

| ITEM | PRICE |
|---|---|
|  |  |
|  |  |
|  |  |
|  |  |
|  |  |
|  |  |
| TOTAL |  |

How much money do you have left over from Month 4?  $_____


Look at the things you bought in month 1. Why did you decide to buy those things first?
_____

Will 4 months be enough time to get everything you want?      YES          NO

If not, how much longer until you can buy everything on your list? _____

# 999 TO ZERO GAME

 2-4 players

 paper and pencil, 3 dice

**Get Ready**

- Each player writes the number 999 at the top of a piece of paper.

**Play**

1. On your turn, decide if you want to roll 1, 2, or 3 dice.

2. Make a number with your dice. Each number is a digit.
For example, if you rolled a 3, 6, and 2, you could make the number 632.

3. Subtract your number from 999.

$$\begin{array}{r} 999 \\ -632 \\ \hline 367 \\ -214 \\ \hline 153 \end{array}$$

4. Take turns rolling and subtracting numbers from your total.

5. As the numbers get smaller, you may need to roll just 1 or 2 dice.

6. If you roll a number that takes you below zero, skip your turn.

7. The first person to get to **zero exactly** wins!

 *Watch a video showing how to play this game at **artfulmath.com/kitten2-goodies**

# WORKING WITH KITTENS

**Volunteering at a Cat Rescue**

**Giving Medicine at the Shelter**

**How to Read Decimals (on Syringes and Other Places)**

**Cat Sitting: "Can You Watch My Cats While I'm Away?"**

**Volunteering with Kittens**

# VOLUNTEERING AT A CAT RESCUE

**Your local cat rescue is looking for volunteers.** You and three of your friends all sign up. The shelter workers are so excited that you will be helping with the cats and kittens!

> **SHELTER WORKER:** Welcome, all of you! Would you like to help socialize the kittens today? We need people to play with them, talk to them, cuddle them, and read to them so they get used to the sound of a human's voice.
>
> **YOU:** Yessss!! That sounds amazing!
>
> **SHELTER WORKER:** Great. We also need help cleaning litter boxes and giving dewormer to the kittens. Are you ok with that?
>
> **YOU:** Of course, we can help with that, too. Anything you need, just let us know.

The four of you create a schedule for **playing, cuddling, and reading to** the cats and kittens. You decide that:

- Every Saturday, each of you will spend **90 minutes** socializing cats and kittens.
- You can do the activities **in any order** (ex: you don't have to do reading first.)
- You and your friends will do each activity at **different times** of the day.
- Each person will spend **more time playing** with the kittens than reading or cuddling.

**In the boxes below, write the times that you and your friends will spend doing each activity.** *Example: 9:00 to 9:30.*

## Kitten Socialization Schedule

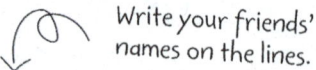
Write your friends' names on the lines.

|  | YOU | _____ | _____ | _____ |
|---|---|---|---|---|
| Reading |  |  |  |  |
| Playing |  |  |  |  |
| Cuddling |  |  |  |  |

# GIVING MEDICINE AT THE SHELTER

It's deworming day! The shelter is giving all the cats a medicine for parasites. There are so many cats and kittens, and the shelter needs your help.

**The directions on the medicine bottle says to give 0.1 mL (one tenth of a milliliter) per pound of a cat's weight. Answer the questions, then round the weights below to the nearest half pound.**

The bottle says to give cats 0.1 mL per pound.

A 3-pound cat would get 0.3 mL of dewormer.

**A 4-pound cat would get _____ mL of dewormer.**

This syringe is divided into tenths:
0.1  0.2  0.3  0.4  etc.

Ten tenths is 1.0 mL, or one milliliter.

**How many mLs of medicine is in this syringe?   0.3   0.4   0.5**

---

The shelter worker tells you to **round down** the cats' weights to the nearest **half pound**.

**DON'T ROUND UP.**

---

One pound = 16 ounces
½ pound = 8 ounces

9 pounds 10 ounces rounds down to 9 ½ lbs.

10 pounds 2 ounces rounds down to _____ lbs.

---

By rounding the weights **down**, you make sure you don't give kittens and cats too much medicine.

---

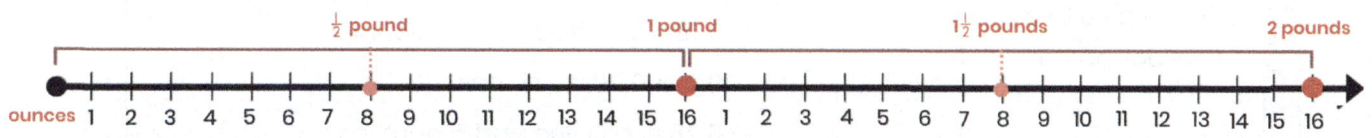

**Round these cats' weights down to the nearest POUND or HALF POUND.**

One pound = 16 oz, so ½ pound = _____ oz.

Whenever you see between 8 and 15 ounces, that will round down to a half pound.

| Luna (Siamese, female) | Tiger (Ragdoll kitten, male) | Maisie (Persian, female) |
|---|---|---|
| 8 lbs 12 oz | 2 lbs 4 oz | 10 lbs 10 oz |
| Rounded down: 8 ½ lbs | Rounded down: _____ lbs | Rounded down: _____ lbs |
| **Dexter (black kitten, male)** | **Sammy (orange tabby, male)** | **Bumble (grey tabby, female)** |
| 4 lbs 15 oz | 12 lbs 6 oz | 9 lbs 13 oz |
| Rounded down: _____ lbs | Rounded down: _____ lbs | Rounded down: _____ lbs |

# HOW TO READ DECIMALS (ON SYRINGES AND OTHER PLACES)

**Decimals are a way to talk about parts of things.** They are like fractions that way.

A medicine syringe holds one milliliter. **It is divided into tenths**, so we can give cats and kittens just a small part of one milliliter.

A 4-pound cat gets 0.4 (four tenths) mL of dewormer.

A 2-pound cat gets _____ (or two tenths) mL of dewormer.

A 6-pound cat gets _____ (or six _____ ) mL of dewormer.

An 8-pound cat gets _____ (or _____ _____ ) mL of dewormer.

**What if you have a cat that is 5 and a HALF pounds? What decimal do you use then?**

Color in the syringe to show how much medicine you would give to a 5 ½ pound cat.

When you are reading decimals, the **first** number after the dot is called "**tenths**". The **second** number after the dot is called "**hundredths**".

Decimals make more sense if you think of them like money. Tenths are like dimes. Hundredths are like pennies.

**0.1** or **0.10** = one dime
**0.15** = one dime and 5 pennies
**0.2** or **0.20** = 2 dimes
**0.25** = 2 dimes and 5 pennies
**0.3** or **0.30** = 3 dimes
**0.35** = 3 dimes and 5 pennies

**Fill in the blanks to complete the counting pattern with decimals.**

0.4    0.45    0.5    _____    0.6    _____    0.7    _____    _____    0.85

**Look at the syringe that you colored in with the dosage for the 5 ½ pound cat.**

**How would you write that amount as a decimal?** _____

**"Would you mind giving dewormer to these kittens?"** asks the shelter worker. **"Sure!"** you reply. She assures you that these syringes do not have needles. You will give the medicine by mouth.

Use the table at the bottom of the page to figure out how much medicine (the "dosage") to give each kitten. **Color in the syringe, starting at the tip, to show the correct dose.**

Round weights down to the nearest half pound. (NOTE: 0.15 is halfway between 0.1 and 0.2)

Bumpkin (Tabby, male)
3 lbs 6 oz
Rounded down:
_____ lbs

Dosage: _____ mL

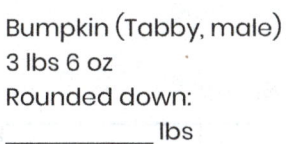

Mia (Ragdoll, female)
4 lbs 15 oz
Rounded down:
_____ lbs

Dosage: _____ mL

Zuzu (White Rex, male)
6 lbs 4 oz
Rounded down:
_____ lbs

Dosage: _____ mL

Bo (Tabby, male)
6 lbs 13 oz
Rounded down:
_____ lbs

Dosage: _____ mL

Tabitha (Siamese, female)
4 lbs 9 oz
Rounded down:
_____ lbs

Dosage: _____ mL

Tidbit (Orange, female)
2 lbs 11 oz
Rounded down:
_____ lbs

Dosage: _____ mL

| POUNDS | DOSAGE |
|---|---|
| 1 pound | 0.1 mL |
| 1 ½ pounds | 0.15 mL |
| 2 pounds | 0.2 mL |
| 2 ½ pounds | 0.25 mL |
| 3 pounds | 0.3 mL |
| 3 ½ pounds | 0.35 mL |

| POUNDS | DOSAGE |
|---|---|
| 4 pounds | 0.4 mL |
| 4 ½ pounds | 0.45 mL |
| 5 pounds | 0.5 mL |
| 5 ½ pounds | 0.55 mL |
| 6 pounds | 0.6 mL |
| 6 ½ pounds | 0.65 mL |

| POUNDS | DOSAGE |
|---|---|
| 7 pounds | 0.7 mL |
| 7 ½ pounds | 0.75 mL |
| 8 pounds | 0.8 mL |
| 8 ½ pounds | 0.85 mL |
| 9 pounds | 0.9 mL |
| 9 ½ pounds | 0.95 mL |

# CAT SITTING: "CAN YOU WATCH MY CATS WHILE I'M AWAY?"

Your neighbor is going on vacation, and asks if you would mind taking care of her cats. "Sure, I'd love that!" you tell her. "Your neighbor says, **"Great! How much do you charge?"**

Hmmm...good question! First you'll find out what other people charge, then you'll decide on your rates. **Read the notes from your research, then write your prices in the chart below.**

### CAT SITTING NOTES

The average rate for cat sitters is $25-$60 per day. Charge a lower rate if just starting out.

Add-ons like brushing and play sessions are a one-time fee, not charged daily.

Clipping claws is hard! Charge at least 1/4 of your basic daily rate for clipping claws.

(If basic rate is $24 per day, clipping claws could be $6.)

### PRICE CHART FOR CAT SITTING

| | Service | Price |
|---|---|---|
| **Basic Daily Rate (1 or 2 cats)** | Visit 15 minutes twice a day; feed and clean litter boxes | per day |
| | price for each additional cat (3 cats or more) | per day |
| **Optional Add-ons** | half hour play session | per day |
| | clip claws | |
| | brushing | |
| | water plants | |

**Use your price chart to answer the questions below:**

How much would a neighbor pay you to take care of her 2 cats for 3 days? (Just basic care, no extra add-ons.) _____

One neighbor says, "I have one cat, and I'll be gone for 4 days. Fluffy has long fur, so she will need to be brushed. How much do I owe you?" they ask. You say: _____

Your next-door neighbor asks you to watch their 3 cats for 5 days. They also want you to water their plants. "How much does that come to?" they ask. You say: _____

Your best friend's parents have 3 cats. They ask you to cat sit for 8 days, with play sessions. You give them a 50% "friends and family" discount. How much do you charge? _____

**Fill in your prices from the previous page. Read the notes and fill out a form for each customer. Write each customer's total cost for cat sitting.**

Customer:_____ Dates traveling: _____ to _____

| Services | Select | Price | How many days? | Subtotal |
|---|---|---|---|---|
| Basic rate (1-2 cats) | ☐ | | | |
| How many additional cats? ____ | ☐ | | | |
| Half hour play session | ☐ | | | |
| Brushing | ☐ | | --- | |
| Clip Claws | ☐ | | --- | |
| Water Plants | ☐ | | --- | |
| | | | | TOTAL |

**CUSTOMER: Mrs. Gupta**
**NUMBER OF CATS: 3**
**DATES: August 3 – 7**
**ADD-ON SERVICES:**
- 30 minute play session
- water plants

**CUSTOMER: Jim McNab**
**NUMBER OF CATS: 5**
**DATES: July 12 – 18**
**ADD-ON SERVICES:**
- brush
- clip claws

Customer:_____ Dates traveling: _____ to _____

| Services | Select | Price | How many days? | Subtotal |
|---|---|---|---|---|
| Basic rate (1-2 cats) | ☐ | | | |
| How many additional cats? ____ | ☐ | | | |
| Half hour play session | ☐ | | | |
| Brushing | ☐ | | --- | |
| Clip Claws | ☐ | | --- | |
| Water Plants | ☐ | | --- | |
| | | | | TOTAL |

Customer:_____ Dates traveling: _____ to _____

| Services | Select | Price | How many days? | Subtotal |
|---|---|---|---|---|
| Basic rate (1-2 cats) | ☐ | | | |
| How many additional cats? ____ | ☐ | | | |
| Half hour play session | ☐ | | | |
| Brushing | ☐ | | --- | |
| Clip Claws | ☐ | | --- | |
| Water Plants | ☐ | | --- | |
| | | | | TOTAL |

**CUSTOMER: Marjory Lin**
**NUMBER OF CATS: 6**
**DATES: Sept 1 – 12**
**ADD-ON SERVICES:**
- play sessions
- clip claws
- water plants

# VOLUNTEERING WITH KITTENS

You love your kittens so much, and you're so grateful you got them—but you keep thinking about all the other kittens who are still waiting to be adopted.

"What can I do to help cats and kittens without a home?" you ask. Your parents sit down with you to brainstorm and think of ways you might help kittens in shelters.

You made a list of a bunch of things kids can do to help kittens. **Put a check by each one you might like to do:**

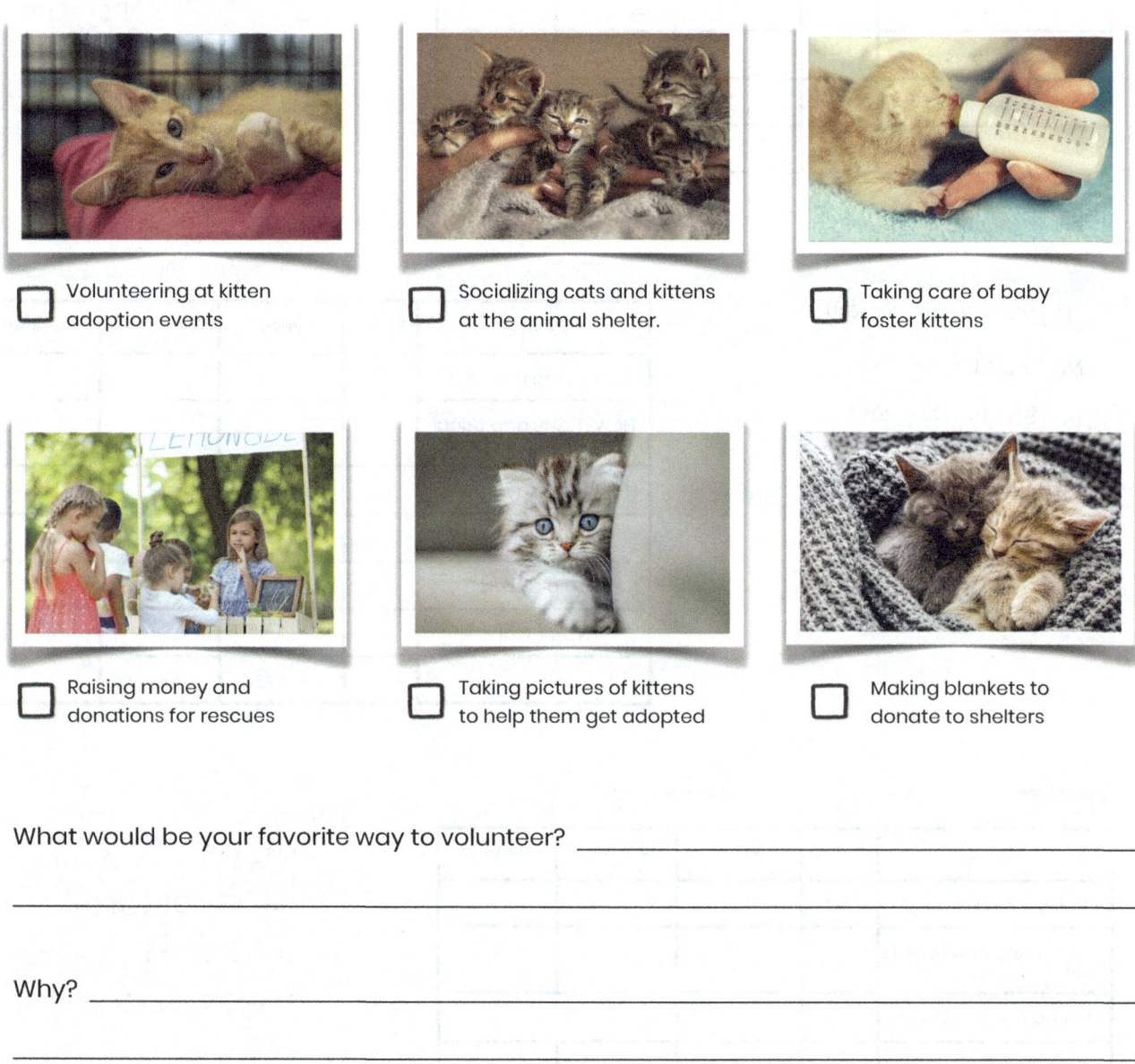

☐ Volunteering at kitten adoption events

☐ Socializing cats and kittens at the animal shelter.

☐ Taking care of baby foster kittens

☐ Raising money and donations for rescues

☐ Taking pictures of kittens to help them get adopted

☐ Making blankets to donate to shelters

What would be your favorite way to volunteer? _____
_____

Why? _____
_____

What friends would you want to volunteer with you? _____
_____

# KITTEN BLANKET GAME

   2-4 players

   game board (page 108), 2 dice, markers

1. Give each player their own game board and a marker.

2. Roll two dice. Is the total ODD or EVEN?

### ODD
**Choose ONE** of the dice numbers.
Decide if it will be **tenths** or **hundredths**.
Color in that much of your board.

### EVEN
You must use **BOTH dice numbers**
to make a decimal number in the
**hundredths**. Color in that many squares.

**This player rolled a 7—an odd number.**
They choose to use the 4.
They color in 0.4, or four tenths.

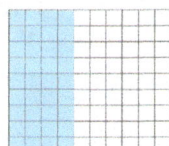

**This player rolled a 6—an even number.**
They must use both digits.
They color in 0.51, or fifty-one hundredths.

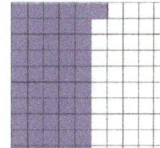

Tenths are ONE WHOLE ROW.
There are 10 rows on a blanket...

Hundredths are ONE SMALL SQUARE.
There are 100 squares on a blanket.

3. The players **must get an exact number** to finish the blanket. If you roll a number you cannot use, skip that turn.

4. The first player to finish their kitten blanket wins!

 *Get printable game boards and videos of how to play at **artfulmath.com/kitten2-goodies**

# HAPPY BIRTHDAY, KITTENS!

Plan Your Kittens' Birthday Party

Make a Party Schedule

How Will You Cut the Birthday Cake?

Make a Dance Playlist

Kitten-Themed Goody Bags

# PLAN YOUR KITTENS' BIRTHDAY PARTY

You can hardly believe it: your kittens are turning ONE YEAR OLD! 🤯
You decide to throw them a fun birthday party, and invite all your kitten-loving friends.

**Answer the questions below to plan the details of your kittens' party.**

**1** You need 15 feet of streamers to decorate. If each pack contains 4 feet of streamers. How many packs will you need? _____

What if each pack contains 3 feet of streamers? _____

**2** You plan to decorate the table with kitten postcards and toy mice.

You want 2 toy mice for every postcard. If you have 13 postcards, how many toy mice do you need?

_____ toy mice

**3** Six of your friends live close enough that you can walk to their house to deliver their invitations. It's about 120 feet between each house..

How many feet will you walk to drop off their invitations? _____ feet

**4** You plan to leave the house at 10:40am to go shopping. You'll need 35 minutes at the store, 15 minutes at the bakery, and 10 minutes to walk home.

What time will you get back?
_____

**5** You need 25 balloons. There are 6 in a pack. Each pack costs $2.75.

How much will you spend on balloons?
_____

Will one $10 bill be enough?
   YES      NO

**6** You're making a music playlist for the party. Most of the songs are a little under 4 minutes long.

About how many songs will you need to fill 30 minutes?

_____ songs

**7** Each guest will get 5 cute cat stickers in their goody bag.

There are 20 stickers per sticker sheet. How many sticker sheets should you buy if you're inviting 10 guests?

_____ sticker sheets

**8** You bake 3 trays of cupcakes. Each tray has 6 cupcakes. 1/2 of the total have chocolate frosting. Two cupcakes have vanilla frosting. The rest have strawberry.

How many have chocolate? _____
How many have strawberry? _____

# MAKE A PARTY SCHEDULE

This party is going to be so much fun! You've made a list of all the things you need to do on that day, and started to fill in your schedule.

Now you need to fill in the rest of the times on your kitten birthday schedule.

**Read the post-it notes, then write the time that you will do each activity.**

- prep goody bags for 1 hour
- clean house for a half hour
- decorate (hour and a half)
- welcome guests (15 minutes)
- Pin the Tail game (20 minutes)
- snacks (25 minutes)

- cake (20 minutes)
- open presents (25 minutes)
- dance party (30 minutes)
- hand out goody bags (15 min)
- guests leave (10 minutes)
- clean up (45 minutes)

## Kitten Party Schedule

| Time | Activity |
|------|----------|
| 9:00 | Prepare goody bags |
| _____ | Clean house |
| _____ | Decorate |
| 12:00 | PARTY — Welcome guests |
| _____ | Play "Pin the Tail on the Kitten" |
| _____ | Snacks |
| 1:00 | Sing happy birthday, have cake |
| _____ | Open kittens' presents |
| _____ | Dance party! |
| _____ | Hand out goody bags |
| 2:30 | Guests leave, say goodbye |
| _____ | Clean Up |
| _____ | Take a break!!! |
| 5:30 | Dinner |

**How long of a break will you get before dinner?** _____ hours _____ minutes

# HOW WILL YOU CUT THE BIRTHDAY CAKE?

You're feeling a little nervous about cutting the birthday cake...
All your friends will want equal-sized pieces, and they'll all be watching you!

You don't know how many people will be at the party, and you don't want to waste any cake.

**Practice cutting the cake in equal-sized pieces for different numbers of people.**

Cut this cake for 4 people.

Cut for 4 people a different way.

Cut this cake for 6 people.

Cut this cake for 8 people.

Cut this cake for 9 people.

Cut this cake for 12 people.

**You're not sure if your cake will be round or rectangular. Practice cutting these round cakes.**

Cut this cake for 4 people.

Cut this cake for 8 people.

Cut this cake for 16 people.

**Which is easier: cutting a rectangular cake or a round cake?**   RECTANGULAR   ROUND

**Why?** _____

_____

# MAKE A DANCE PLAYLIST

You decide to have music and dancing during some of the birthday party.

The dance party will be 30 minutes long. **Choose songs to fill 30 minutes** (remember to include time for the space between songs), **then write them in the order you want to play them.**

- ✓ There are 2 seconds between each song.
- ✓ Try to fill as much of the 30 minutes as possible.
- ✓ Don't go over 30 minutes.

Look back at your party schedule to see what time the dance party starts!

**The dance party will start at** _____ **and end at** _____,
                                          time                                    time

## SONGS AND PLAY TIMES

| | | |
|---|---|---|
| We Don't Talk About Bruno 3:36 | Dynamite 3:19 | Born This Way 4:20 |
| Dance Monkey 3:29 | Kings & Queens 2:42 | All About That Bass 3:07 |
| Happy 3:52 | Sucker 3:01 | Roar 3:43 |
| Sunroof 2:43 | Can't Stop the Feeling 3:57 | Handclap 3:13 |
| Feel It Still 2:43 | Watch Me 3:05 | Waka Waka 3:19 |
| Sunshine 2:43 | Uptown Funk 4:29 | Despacito 3:49 |
| On Top of the World 3:09 | Cheap Thrills 3:44 | Cha Cha Slide 6:27 |
| Gangam Style 3:39 | Gummy Bear Song 3:10 | Hamster Dance 3:32 |

| | song | start time | song length | end time | add two seconds |
|---|---|---|---|---|---|
| 1 | | | | | |
| 2 | | | | | |
| 3 | | | | | |
| 4 | | | | | |
| 5 | | | | | |
| 6 | | | | | |
| 7 | | | | | |
| 8 | | | | | |

# MAKE KITTEN-THEMED GOODY BAGS FOR YOUR GUESTS

Everyone who comes to your kittens' birthday party will take home a goody bag of prizes! **You will need to buy enough prizes for 17 bags. List the prizes you will buy on the next page, then add up the total. You have $100 to spend.**

✓ Each bag should have at least 4 different prizes.
✓ Each bag includes 5 stickers.
✓ All the bags have the same types of prizes inside.

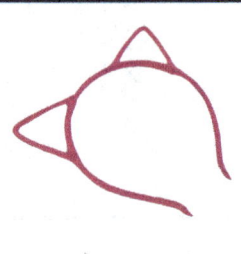

**Cat Ears Headband**

Set of 10 headbands, plastic, assorted colors.

**$8.00**

**Cute Kitten Notebooks**

Adorable mini-notebooks with kittens. Set of 3.

**$3.99**

**Small Cat Squishy Toy**

Includes 4 fat cats in various colors per pack.

**$4.50**

**Candy Necklaces**

Package of 3 paw print candy necklaces.

**$1.00**

**Glamour Kitty Keychains**

Fancy jeweled princess cat keychains. Set of 2.

**$4.25**

**Cat Slap Bracelets**

Fun, cartoony cat illustrations. 6 bracelets

**$8.95**

**Jeweled Cat Necklace**

Lightweight, cute kitten necklace for kids.

**$1.50**

**Cat-Shaped Notepads**

Small cat notepads in bright colors, set of 6.

**$7.99**

**Kitten Erasers**

Set of 10 pencil top erasers in mixed colors.

**$5.50**

**Chocolate Candies**

Cat-themed chocolates. Package of 20 candies.

**$3.50**

**Lucky Cat Toy**

This tiny cat companion fits in your pocket.

**$1.00**

**Cat Sticker Sheets**

2 sheets per set. 20 stickers per sheet.

**$3.99**

**You have $100 to spend on goody bags. Write each item and quantity below and find the total.**

| ITEM | HOW MANY IN EACH PACKAGE | PRICE | QUANTITY | TOTAL PRICE |
|---|---|---|---|---|
|  |  |  |  |  |
|  |  |  |  |  |
|  |  |  |  |  |
|  |  |  |  |  |
|  |  |  |  |  |
|  |  |  |  |  |
|  |  |  | GRAND TOTAL |  |

**Draw a picture of one complete goody bag, with all the prizes each person will get.**

How much did you spend on goody bags altogether? _____

How much money did you have left over? _____

How much is each goody bag worth? _____

Will you have extra prizes left over?   YES   NO

What will you do with any leftover prizes? _____

_____

# PIN THE TAIL ON THE KITTEN

 2 players

 game boards and kitten cutout (pages 109–112), tape

### Get Ready

- **Decide who will be the HIDER and who will be the GUESSER.**
  (The "hider" will hide the kitten. The "guesser" will try to find it.)

- Give each player a **game board** from pages 109 and 110.

- **Cut out the kitten body and tail** on page 112. Give the kitten body to the "hider". Give the tail to the "guesser".

- Sit **back-to-back** with the other player.

- The "hider" tapes the kitten body anywhere on their game board grid. **The X on the kitten butt must be at the intersection of two crossed lines.**

The X of this kitten's butt is right where lines (2, 1) cross. This is called the "intersection" of two lines.

### Play

1. **The guesser will try to guess where the tail goes (kitten butt X).** The guesser calls out two numbers—for example, "two, four!"

— The first number is the HORIZONTAL line (across).
— The second number is for the VERTICAL line (up and down).

These numbers are called **coordinates**. Coordinates help you find an exact spot on a grid.

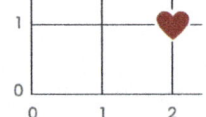

The heart on this grid is at coordinates 1 , 2

2. If the guesser lands on **the kitten's body**, the hider says, "**PURR**".
If their guess lands **outside of the kitten's body**, the hider says, "**HISS**".
If they guess the **exact spot where the kitten's butt X is**, the hider says, "**MEOW!**"

3. Once they guess the exact spot, the guesser **pins their tail** on the other player's game board.

**Switch places and play again** so the other person can be the guesser.

 *Get printable game boards and videos of how to play at **artfulmath.com/kitten2-goodies**

# LET'S START A KITTEN CLUB

**Club Activity 1: Cat Eye Colors**

**Club Activity 2: Cat Symmetry**

**Club Activity 3: Cool Cat Facts**

**Club Activity 4: The Average Weight of Cats**

**Club Activity 5: The Orange Cat Game**

**Club Activity 6: How to Draw a Kitten**

# LET'S START A KITTEN CLUB!

You and your friends decide to start a club for kids who love kittens.

"**Let's just do cat things!**" says one friend.

"Yeah! And we can **learn all about cats and kittens**," says another.

"Can we **play games**?" asks another. "**We'll have so much fun!!**"

You and your friends will take turns coming up with fun kitten activities for your club members to do together. But first, you need to make your club OFFICIAL. 🐱

**Write the name of your club and the kids in the club, and make a sign for your clubhouse.**

CLUB NAME: _____

CLUB MEMBERS:

_____    _____
_____    _____
_____    _____
_____    _____

CLUB SIGN:

Put a check by the things you want to do in your club:

- ☐ Learn about cats and kittens
- ☐ Learn to draw kittens
- ☐ Play fun games
- ☐ Do cat and kitten activities
- ☐ Other: _____

# CLUB ACTIVITY 1: CAT EYE COLORS

"What's your favorite eye color for cats?" asks one of the kids in your club.
Everyone starts talking at once: "Blue eyes!" "Gold!" "I like black cats with green eyes!"

"I have an idea! Let's draw all the possible combinations of black, brown, and orange kittens with green, gold, or blue eyes!"

Color all the possible combinations of black, brown, and orange kittens with green, gold, or blue eyes.

How many different combinations did you find? _____

Which combination did you like best? Circle your favorite!

# CLUB ACTIVITY 2: CAT SYMMETRY

"Did you know, many cats have faces that are SYMMETRICAL?" a club member says.

"What's 'smametical' mean?" asks the youngest kid in your group.

Everyone laughs. "Not smametical! SYMMETRICAL means when both sides look the same. Both sides have the same colors and patterns, like a mirror image."

**Circle each kitten or cat with a symmetrical face.**

**Draw a heart ❤️ next to your favorite SYMMETRICAL cat face.**

**Draw a happy face 😊 next to your favorite NON-SYMMETRICAL cat face.**

Do you know a cat in real life who has a symmetrical face? Write its name: _____

Do you know a cat in real life with a non-symmetrical face? Write its name: _____

Color in this kitten's face with markings that **are symmetrical.**

Give this kitten markings that are **NOT symmetrical.**

# CLUB ACTIVITY 3: COOL CAT FACTS

Another club member LOVES telling everyone fun facts about cats and kittens—so they made a matching game for today's club activity. **Draw a line to match each cat fact to its answer.**

A female kitten can **get pregnant** as young as _____ months old.
520 - 516

• 15

The **oldest** known cat, Creme Puff, lived to be _____ years old.
20 x 2 - 2

• 20

Cats **sleep** an average of _____ hours per day.
1220 - 1205

• 30

Cats can **jump** _____ times their own height.
20 ÷ 4

• 4

People began keeping cats as **pets** as long as _____ years ago.
4500 + 4500 + 500

• 38

Cats can make _____ different **sounds** that mean different things.
800 - 100 + 20 - 700

• 9,500

A domestic cat can **run** up to _____ miles per hour over short distances.
3 x 5 + 115 - 100

• 5

# CLUB ACTIVITY 4: THE AVERAGE WEIGHT OF CATS

"**I heard that Maine Coons are really big!**" says another club member. "**Let's find the average weight of different kinds of cats!**"

"**Cats aren't average!**" the youngest club member protests. "**Cats are amazing!**"

Another club member says, "Don't worry, we're not saying cats are average! The **average weight** means **about how much that kind of cat usually weighs.**"

"Maine Coons don't all weigh exactly the same. But if you weighed a hundred Maine Coons, most of them would be a similar weight. We call that their *average weight*."

"**But how do you find the average?**" someone asks. One of your friends explains:

| Name | Breed | Weight |
|---|---|---|
| Gigi | Maine Coon | 19 lbs |
| Leo | Maine Coon | 22 lbs |
| Midnight | Maine Coon | 20 lbs |
| Oliver | Maine Coon | 15 lbs |

Gigi, Leo, Midnight, and Oliver are all Maine Coon cats. **They weigh 19 pounds, 22 pounds, 20 pounds, and 15 pounds.**

Let's find the **average weight** of these four Maine Coon cats:

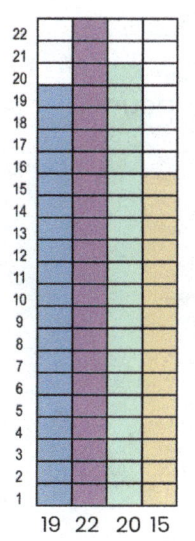

This graph shows the weights of the four Maine Coons.

**Imagine these are four stacks of blocks.**

Now move the blocks around so all the stacks are the same size.

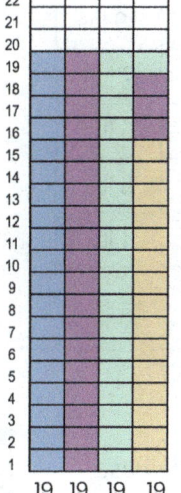

After sharing the "blocks" equally, they now all show the same weight: 19 pounds.

**This new number (19) is the AVERAGE weight of all four Maine Coon cats.** We can say "Maine Coons weigh *about* 19 pounds."

---

**Division** is a quick way to "share the blocks" equally and find the average.

1. Add all the weights together: 15 + 22 + 19 + 20 = _____

2. Divide the total by the number of cats.   4⟌76

3. The average weight of the four Maine Coons is _____ lbs.

One of your friends asks, "**Which cat breeds are the biggest? Which cats are the smallest? What is their average size? Let's find out!**"

Together, you find the weights of different breeds of cats, and organize them into a chart. **Now you can use division to find the average weights of the different cat breeds.**

| Name | Breed | Weight |
|---|---|---|
| Luna | Siamese | 8 lbs |
| Mochi | Siamese | 11 lbs |
| Loki | Siamese | 7 lbs |
| Buttercup | Siamese | 10 lbs |
| Gigi | Maine Coon | 15 lbs |
| Leo | Maine Coon | 22 lbs |
| Midnight | Maine Coon | 19 lbs |
| Oliver | Maine Coon | 20 lbs |
| Momo | American Shorthair | 12 lbs |
| Sadie | American Shorthair | 11 lbs |
| Shadow | American Shorthair | 8 lbs |
| Bella | American Shorthair | 9 lbs |
| Nala | Ragdoll | 11 lbs |
| Mimi | Ragdoll | 17 lbs |
| Tilly | Ragdoll | 13 lbs |
| Pumpkin | Ragdoll | 19 lbs |
| Boo | Singapura | 7 lbs |
| Mia | Singapura | 5 lbs |
| Milo | Singapura | 8 lbs |
| Pixie | Singapura | 4 lbs |

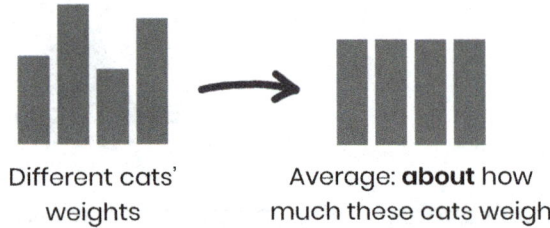

Different cats' weights → Average: **about** how much these cats weigh

1. Choose a cat breed. **Add** all the weights for that cat breed.
2. **Divide** the total by the number of cats (4).
3. The answer to the division problem is the **average weight** of those four cats.

**What is the average weight of:**

**Siamese?** _____ pounds

**Maine Coon?** _____ pounds

**American Shorthair?** _____ pounds

**Ragdoll?** _____ pounds

**Singapura?** _____ pounds

Use the data from the previous page to fill in the bar graph of average weights.
**Start at the bottom, and color in each bar to show the average weight of each breed.**

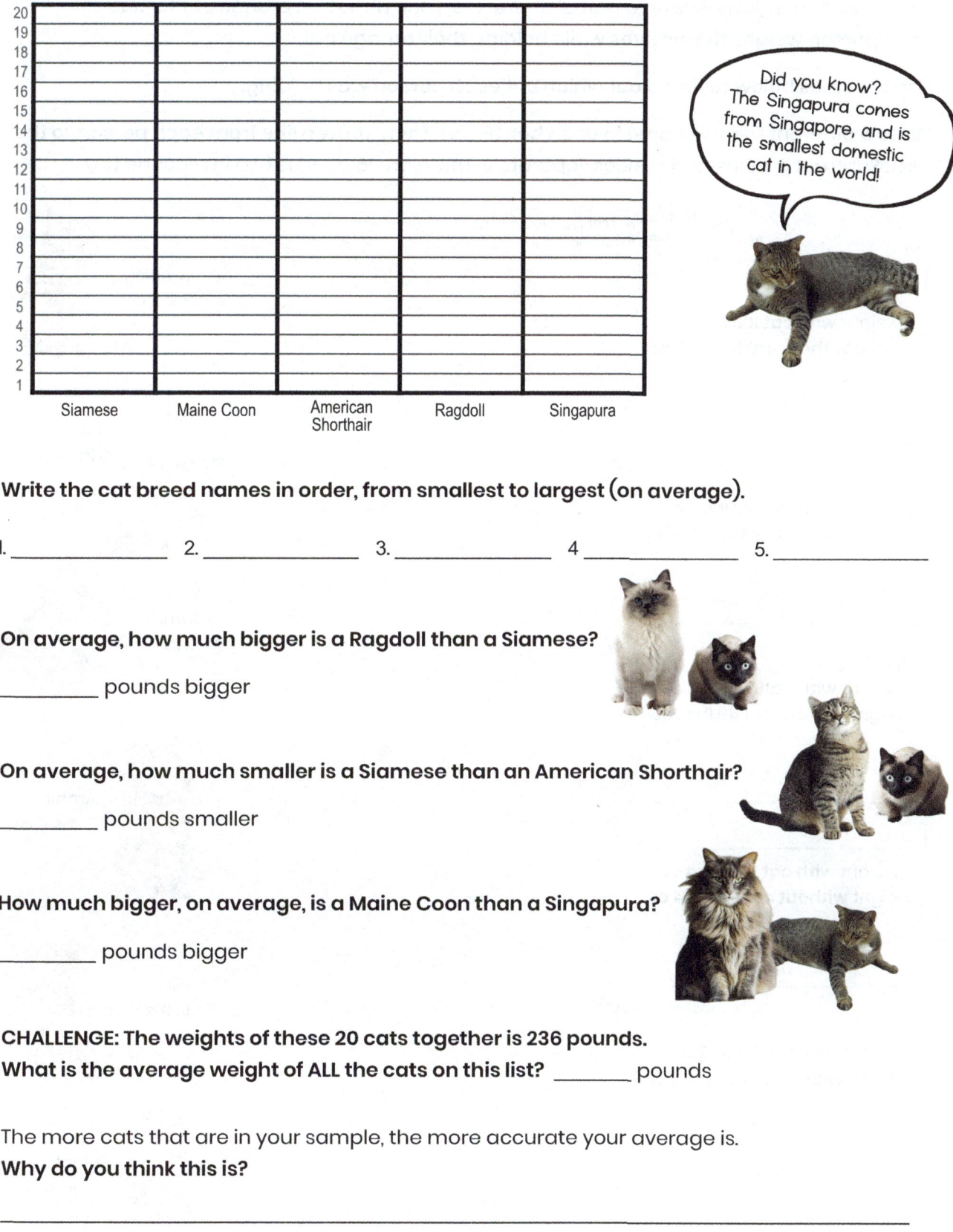

**Write the cat breed names in order, from smallest to largest (on average).**

1. _____  2. _____  3. _____  4 _____  5. _____

**On average, how much bigger is a Ragdoll than a Siamese?**

_____ pounds bigger

**On average, how much smaller is a Siamese than an American Shorthair?**

_____ pounds smaller

**How much bigger, on average, is a Maine Coon than a Singapura?**

_____ pounds bigger

**CHALLENGE: The weights of these 20 cats together is 236 pounds.
What is the average weight of ALL the cats on this list?** _____ pounds

The more cats that are in your sample, the more accurate your average is.
**Why do you think this is?**

_____
_____

# CLUB ACTIVITY 5: THE ORANGE CAT GAME

One of your friends makes up a game where everyone brings an orange cat to club. **Each person weighs themselves while holding their orange cat.**

**Use the clues below to figure out which cat each person was holding.**

**Write a different friend's name in each box below. Then draw a line from each person to their cat.**
HINT: Subtract pounds and ounces separately. There are 16 ounces (oz) in a pound (lb).

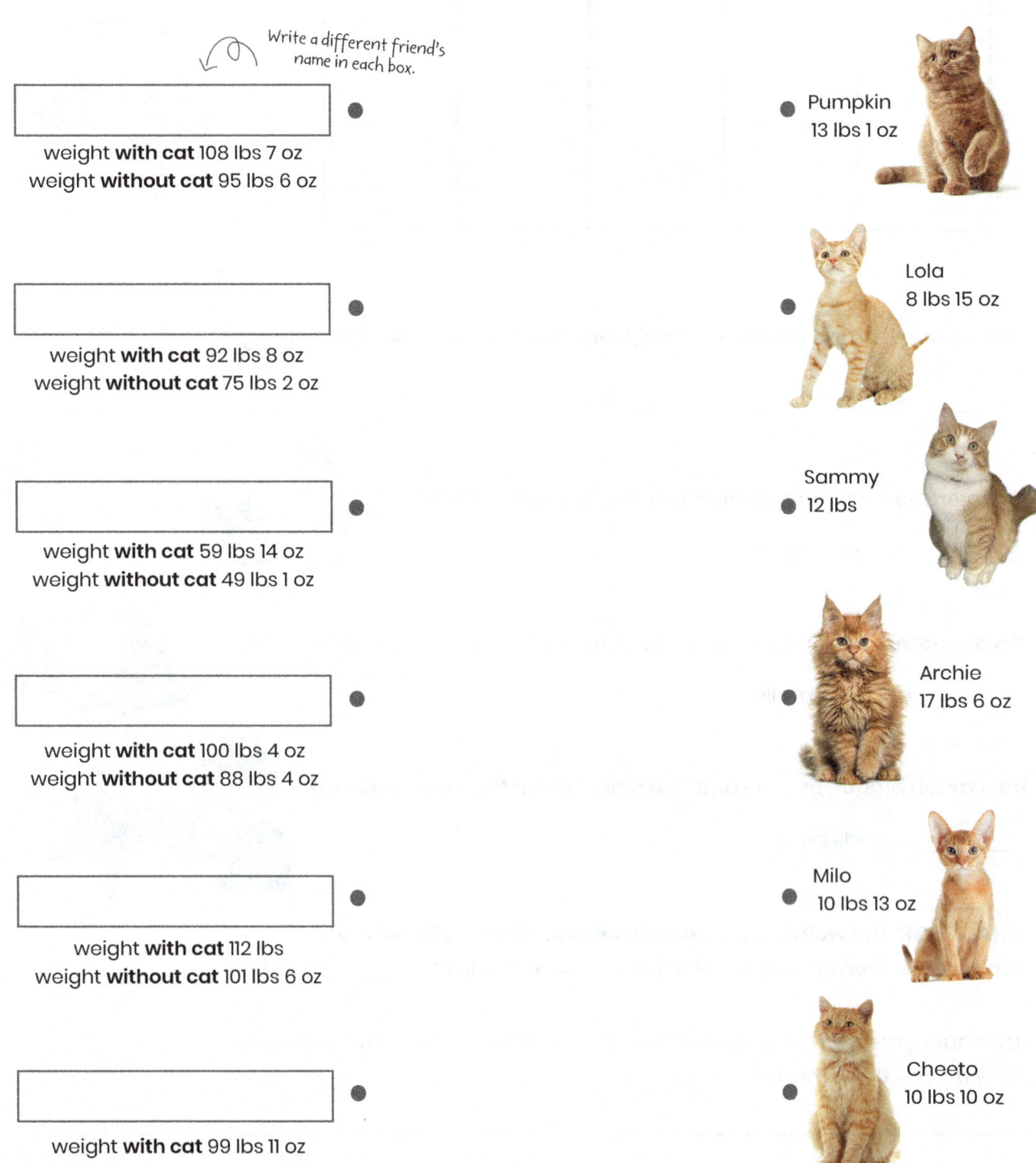

*Write a different friend's name in each box.*

weight **with cat** 108 lbs 7 oz
weight **without cat** 95 lbs 6 oz

weight **with cat** 92 lbs 8 oz
weight **without cat** 75 lbs 2 oz

weight **with cat** 59 lbs 14 oz
weight **without cat** 49 lbs 1 oz

weight **with cat** 100 lbs 4 oz
weight **without cat** 88 lbs 4 oz

weight **with cat** 112 lbs
weight **without cat** 101 lbs 6 oz

weight **with cat** 99 lbs 11 oz
weight **without cat** 90 lbs 12 oz

- Pumpkin 13 lbs 1 oz
- Lola 8 lbs 15 oz
- Sammy 12 lbs
- Archie 17 lbs 6 oz
- Milo 10 lbs 13 oz
- Cheeto 10 lbs 10 oz

# CLUB ACTIVITY 6: HOW TO DRAW A KITTEN

One kid in club says she wants to learn how to draw kittens. "Cats and kittens all look the same when I draw them," she says. "**How do I make it look more kitten-y?**"

All of you look closely at cats' and kittens' faces for awhile You find a library book that explains the difference with pictures and math. **Study the six pictures below of cats and kittens.**

**Which row below shows three kittens?**     TOP ROW     BOTTOM ROW

**Kitten faces look different from grown cats,** and it's not just because kittens are smaller. All the cat and kitten faces in these pictures are the same size.

**What are some differences you notice between a cat's face and a kitten's face?**
(HINT: Compare where the eyes, nose, and mouth are for cats and kittens.)

_____

_____

_____

**Where are the eyes on an adult cat?**     ABOVE the ½ line     BELOW the ½ line     AT the ½ line

**Where are the eyes on a kitten?**     ABOVE the ½ line     BELOW the ½ line     AT the ½ line

**Where is the nose on an adult cat?**     ABOVE the ¼ line     BELOW the ¼ line     AT the ¼ line

**Where is the nose on a kitten?**     ABOVE the ¼ line     BELOW the ¼ line     AT the ¼ line

**Draw two cute kitten faces using the circles below.**
Study the kitten faces on the previous page to see where to draw eyes, nose, and ears.

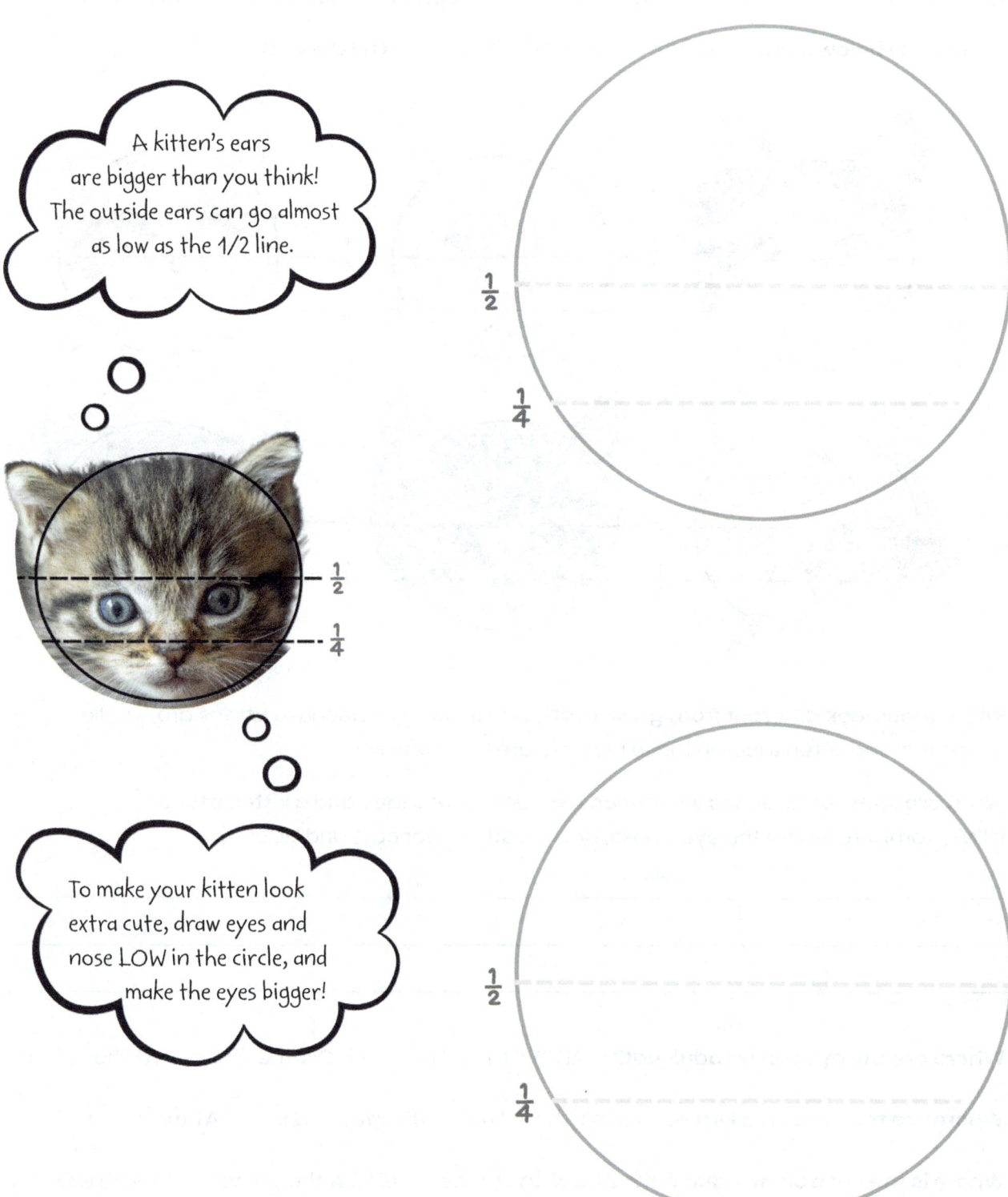

All animals—including human babies—have eyes, nose, and mouth further down their face. The top half of a baby's face is all forehead—just like kittens!

**Math proportions**—such as eyes and nose low down on the face, or big heads on small bodies—are part of what make babies look cute!

How can math proportions help you draw cute baby animals?

_____

_____

_____

# JUST AN AVERAGE GAME

 2-3 players

 deck of cards, paper and pencil

1. Shuffle the cards and remove any jokers from the deck. Aces = 1, Jack = 11, Queen = 12, King = 13.

2. Put the deck face down on the table.

3. On your turn, take at least 3 cards from the deck. You can take as many more cards as you like. **Do not look at the cards as you pick them up**.

4. Find the **average** of all the cards in your hand:

**Add**: 10 + 6 + 5 + 8 = 29
There are 4 cards, so **divide** 29 ÷ 4 = 7 R1

4. Add the total of your cards, then divide by the number of cards you drew.

5. Ignore any remainders. The answer to the division problem is the **average**; write this number as your score.

6. Play until you run out of cards. (Make sure everyone got the same number of turns. If necessary, shuffle the cards so that person can finish the game.)

7. The player with the highest score wins!

 *Get printable game boards and videos of how to play at **artfulmath.com/kitten2-goodies**

# MEET KELLI'S KITTENS

Kazoo

Maisie

Pocky & Pez

## Congratulations—you did it!

Hooray, you completed Kitten Math 2!

Now you know more about kittens and how to take care of them during their first year.

**You've learned so many important skills in both math and kitten care, that you'll use in the real world.**

Minnie

## See all the cute kittens on this page?

I fostered of all these kittens when they were very tiny. (If you want to learn how to take care of tiny kittens, check out my first **Kitten Math** book.)

Two of the kittens on this page—Sammy and Maisie—were my fosters when they were just one week old—with eyes still closed! Later, I adopted both of them so my other kitten Hopey would have some friends.

**Hope, Sammy, and Maisie taught me all about how to take care of growing kittens.** You might say they helped me write this book!

Sammy is the star of **Kitten Math Club** (you're invited!), so he's kind of famous. Sammy sends letters, videos, and fun activities each month to kids in his club!

Calliope

Wren

## Can you find Kelli's kittens in the pages of this book?

Each of the kittens on this page has their picture somewhere in this book. **Can you find them all?**

Rosie

Halloumi

Colby

Sammy

Piccolo

Dexter

Darla & Rascal

# JOIN THE KITTEN MATH CLUB! 🐾

> I, Sammy Fluffcat, hereby invite YOU,
> _____
> (your name here)
> to be part of my super fun and best ever club ONLY for kids who love love love cats!
> I will send you letters and secret messages and puzzles and games and pictures and videos of me doing cool cat things. =^..^=
> I hope you will join my club! Do you want to join my club? Let me know. Meow!!

↳ Sammy Fluffcat

**Meet Sammy—the star of Kitten Math Club!**

You might have seen Sammy in the Kitten Math books. He was just a tiny kitten then. 🐱 Now Sammy is all grown up. He has his very own club…and he wants YOU to join!

Each month, you'll get a letter from Sammy filled with puzzles, a secret code, and fun kitten-club activities. Every challenge hides a clue—collect them all, crack the code, and discover Sammy's message!

## Each month you'll get:

- a letter from Sammy cat
- a funny secret message from Sammy, written in code
- cat-themed puzzles, games, and other fun activities
- photos and videos of Sammy
- monthly cat "sticker" and sticker chart
- BONUS: If you write to Sammy, he will write you back!

→ Join the club at: **bit.ly/kitten-math-club**

# ANSWER KEY

**WHY ADOPT FROM A SHELTER? (pg 6)**
- One mama could give birth to 15 kittens a year!
- Ten female cats could give birth to 150 kittens per year
- In 5 years, ten cats could give birth to 750 kittens

**KITTEN PROOF YOUR HOME (pg 19)**

**PICKING OUT YOUR KITTENS (pg 9):** Look at a calendar and find today's date. Count back 8 weeks to find your kittens' birthdays.

If your kittens have learned 2 new things each day they've been alive, the number of days times 2 = 112 new things they have learned so far.

**KITTEN NAME MATH CODE (pg 11):** Boo Boo: 98, Peanut 85, Squishy 71, Sweetie Pie 154

- PLANTS AND FLOWERS: Always do an online search of "Are (lilies) toxic to cats?" Kittens chew on everything, and they can get very sick if they eat a poisonous plant.

- COFFEE: Keep kittens away from hot drinks. They can spill on kittens and burn them.

- CLEANING SPRAYS have chemicals that can hurt cats. Put these far away.

- RUBBER BANDS, SMALL OBJECTS: Kittens can eat these and need surgery to remove them.

- PLASTIC BAGS: Kittens can crawl inside, get tangled up, and suffocate.

- CHOCOLATE is poisonous to cats and dogs.

- CORDS: Kittens chew on cords and destroy them. They can also get tangled up in long cords, or electrocuted if cords are plugged in.

- YARN is very dangerous to cats because they swallow it and it gets tangled up with their insides. Always put yarn or string away when you are not using it.

**SHARING KITTEN RESPONSIBILITIES (pg 21):** Each person will spend 90 minutes on kitten care. Here is one possible solution:

- **Person 1:** feed breakfast (5), clean litter boxes (10), clip claws (20), take to vet (40), hide treats at night (15).

- **Person 2:** play with kittens – morning (30), brush kittens (25), feed lunch (5), feed dinner (5), play with kittens – evening (25)

## WHAT ARE YOUR KITTENS' PURR-SONALITIES? (pg 25)
- Mr. McFuzz: crazy, silly, confident, fearless
- Sweet Pea: sensitive, gentle, shy
- Both kittens: cuddly, happy, curious

## HOW DO YOUR KITTENS LIKE TO BE PETTED? (pg 27)
What would be your score if you pet your kitten's CHIN, TAIL, and HEAD? 9 points

| | | | |
|---|---|---|---|
| Taylor +10 points | Sam +1 point | Sabina +17 points | Ari −5 points |
| Mika −20 points | Ryan +13 points | Keisha −7 points | Larry +9 points |

Sabina was best at petting.   Mika was worst at petting.

## HOW MUCH DO YOUR KITTENS EAT? (pg 37)
- Two kittens eat at least 12 ounces food per day
- Four 3-oz cans per day
- You need 28 3-oz cans per week (4x7)
- You need 120 cans per month (4x30)
- 10 cans last 2 1/2 days (4+4+2)
- You'll need to buy food on Sunday
- Sammy ate 8 oz, Maisie ate 7 oz

## HOW MUCH MEAT DO THESE FOODS HAVE? (pg 39)
1. "feast" 25%
2. "flavors" less than 3%
3. "with" 3%
4. "entree" 25% ("Entree" is a French word for 'meal')
5. "recipe" 25%
6. "flavors" less than 3%

## BE A KITTEN FOOD DETECTIVE (pg 38)

If it says "dinner", "recipe", "entree", "formula" or "feast", it's at least 25% meat

You might see cat food called Chicken Dinner, Fish Recipe, Beef Formula, and so on. These words tell you that **at least 25% of the ingredients are meat** (between 25% and 95%).

COLOR IN 25 BOXES TO SHOW THE **MINIMUM AMOUNT** OF MEAT IN EACH CAN OF FOOD

If you see the word "with" in the title (such as "with chicken"), it has at least 3% meat

If you see the word "with" in the name, that means it has **at least 3 percent meat** (between 3% and 25%.) They are trying to trick you into thinking the food has a lot of meat, when it doesn't.

COLOR IN 3 BOXES TO SHOW THE **MINIMUM AMOUNT** OF MEAT IN EACH CAN OF FOOD

If you see the word "flavor" in the name, that means it has LESS than 3% meat!

The word "flavor" just means "taste". If a bag or can says "flavor", there is almost no meat inside! Don't be fooled by fancy packaging. Look for clues to what's really inside.

COLOR IN 1 OR 2 BOXES TO SHOW WHAT LESS THAN 3% LOOKS LIKE

## THE FIRST 5 INGREDIENTS TRICK
- Which ingredient is there MOST of? chicken
- Does this label look like a healthy food? YES—the first ingredients are mostly meat
- What might be the name of this food? Chicken Dinner for Kittens
- After chicken, the second ingredient is chicken broth
- The ingredient that has HALF the amount as chicken broth is egg (20% and 10%)

## WHICH FOODS GET THE HIGHEST SCORE? (pg 41)
1. 2 + 2 + 2 + 0 + 0 = 6
2. 2 + 0 + 2 + 2 + 2 = 8
3. −2 + 0 − 2 − 2 + 0 = −6
4. 2 + 2 + 2 + 0 + 0 = 6
5. 2 + 2 + 2 + 2 − 2 = 8
6. 0 − 2 − 2 − 2 + 0 = −6
7. 0 + 2 − 2 + 0 + 2 = 2
8. 2 + 0 + 2 + 2 + 2 = 8
9. −2 + 0 − 2 − 2 + 0 = −6
10. 2 + 2 + 2 + 0 + 0 = 6

**Best:** 2, 5, 8
**Worst:** 3, 6, 9

Wet food is better because cats don't drink much water. They get their water from food. When the food is dry, cats don't get enough water and can get dehydrated.

### BUYING KITTEN FOOD (pg 43)
- 1 month = 120 cans
- Cost = $120 (rounded up)
- 3/4 of $120 = $90. You saved $30. You have $10 left over.
- 3/4 of $20 = $15. You save $5.
- 3/4 of $44 = $33. You save $11.

### BUYING KITTEN FOOD (pg 44)
- small can
- Kitten Yum
- 5-pound bag

### WHICH KITTEN IS MORE PLAYFUL? (pg 48)
- Kitten 1 woke you up in the middle of the night (1:40am to 2:40am played on your bed)
- Kitten 2 played in a paper bag for 15 minutes
- Kitten 1 played in a cardboard box for 50 minutes
- Kitten 1 spent more time acting crazy with zoomies (35 minutes, vs. Kitten 2 — 30 minutes)
- How many minutes did Kitten 1 play? 165 minutes, or 2 hours 45 minutes
- How many minutes did Kitten 2 play? 150 minutes, or 2 hours 30 minutes
- Which kitten played more? Kitten 1 -  How much more? 15 minutes

| KITTEN 1 | KITTEN 2 |
|---|---|
| 5:45- 6:20 = 35 minutes | 8:15 - 8:50 = 35 minutes |
| 1:15 - 1:35 = 20 minutes | 11:55 - 12:10 = 15 minutes |
| 5:20 - 6:10 = 50 minutes | 4:15 - 4:40 = 25 minutes |
| 8:55 - 9:30 = 35 minutes | 7:00 - 7:45 = 45 minutes |
| 1:40 - 2:05 = 25 minutes | 9:50 - 10:20 = 30 minutes |
| 165 minutes | 150 minutes |

### HOW HIGH CAN KITTENS JUMP? (pg 49)    —> HINT: Multiply height in inches x 5
1. A 9-inch-tall kitten can jump 45 inches  (3 feet 9 inches)
2. A 5-inch-tall kitten can jump 25 inches  (2 feet 1 inch)
3. A 10-inch-tall kitten can jump 50 inches  (4 feet 2 inches)
4. A 6-inch-tall kitten can jump 30 inches  (2 feet 6 inches)
5. A 7-inch-tall kitten can jump 35 inches  (2 feet 11 inches)
6. A 13-inch-tall kitten can jump 65 inches  (5 feet 5 inches)
7. A 8-inch-tall kitten can jump 40 inches  (3 feet 4 inches)
8. A 12-inch-tall kitten can jump 60 inches  (5 feet exactly)
9. A 14-inch-tall kitten can jump 70 inches  (5 feet 10 inches)
10. A 11-inch-tall kitten can jump 55 inches  (4 feet 7 inches)

### MAKE A KITTEN TOY SCHEDULE (pg 50)
There are many possible solutions. Here is one:

| WEEK 1 | WEEK 2 | WEEK 3 | WEEK 4 | WEEK 5 |
|---|---|---|---|---|
| mouse | crinkle ball | mouse | jingle ball | wand toy |
| jingle ball | spring | kicker toy | spring | crinkle toy |
| puff ball | puzzle toy | tunnel | play mat | puzzle toy |
| kicker toy | play mat | wand toy | puff ball | tunnel |

## WHAT DO YOUR KITTENS NEED? (pg 51)

Cats need wet food because they get most of their **water** from food.

**Scratchers** are important for cats to sharpen claws, stretch, and relieve stress.

Cats need plenty of large, clean **litter** boxes.

**Cat trees** give kittens a place to jump, climb, and play.

Cat beds and **blankets** give kittens a cozy place to sleep.

**Playtime** with kittens helps them practice hunting, bond with you, and have fun.

Different kinds of toys, like **wand toys** and **chaser toys**, keep kittens' bodies and minds healthy.

## WHY DO KITTENS GET IN TROUBLE? (pg 52)

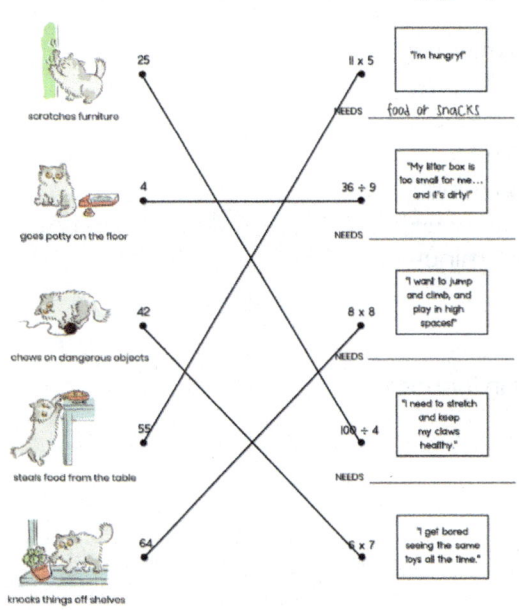

36÷9  Needs: a bigger, clean litter box
8x8  Needs: cat tree
100÷4  Needs: scratching post
6x7  Needs: new toys

## VOLUNTEERING AT A CAT RESCUE (pg 65)

There are many possible solutions. Here is one possibility:

|  | YOU | Marishka | Andrea | Linda |
|---|---|---|---|---|
| Reading | 9:00 - 9:30 | 11:00 - 11:15 | 10:30 - 11:00 | 12:00 - 12:30 |
| Playing | 9:30 - 10:10 | 10:10 - 11:00 | 11:00 - 11:45 | 12:30 - 1:15 |
| Cuddling | 10:10 - 10:30 | 9:45 - 10:10 | 11:45 - 12:00 | 1:15 - 1:30 |

## GIVING MEDICINE AT THE SHELTER (pg 66)

- A 4-pound cat would get 0.4 mL of dewormer
- There are 0.4 mL of medicine in the syringe
- 10 pounds 2 ounces rounds down to 10 pounds
- 1/2 pound = 8 ounces
- Tiger - 2 lbs 4 oz rounds down to 2 pounds
- Maisie - 10 lbs 10 oz rounds down to 10 1/2 pounds
- Dexter - 4 lbs 15 oz rounds down to 4 1/2 pounds
- Sammy - 12 lbs 6 oz rounds down to 12 pounds
- Bumble - 9 lbs 13 oz rounds down to 9 1/2 pounds

## HOW TO READ DECIMALS (pg 67)

- A 2-pound cat gets 0.2 mL (or two tenths) of dewormer
- A 6-pound cat gets 0.6 mL (or six tenths) of dewormer
- An 8-pound cat gets 0.8 mL (or eight tenths) of dewormer
- 0.4, 0.45, 0.5, 0.55, 0.6, 0.65, 0.7, 0.75, 0.8, 0.85
- 0.55

0.55 mL medicine for a 5 1/2 pound cat

## HOW TO READ DECIMALS, CONTINUED (pg 68)

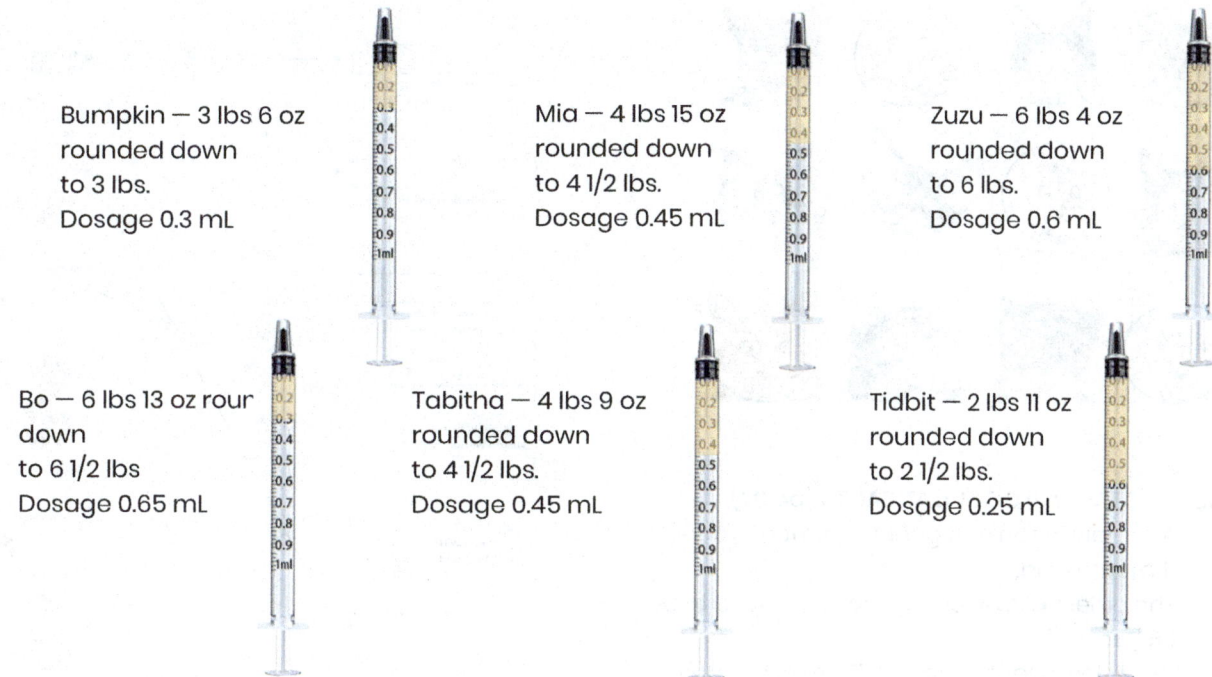

Bumpkin — 3 lbs 6 oz rounded down to 3 lbs. Dosage 0.3 mL

Mia — 4 lbs 15 oz rounded down to 4 1/2 lbs. Dosage 0.45 mL

Zuzu — 6 lbs 4 oz rounded down to 6 lbs. Dosage 0.6 mL

Bo — 6 lbs 13 oz rour down to 6 1/2 lbs Dosage 0.65 mL

Tabitha — 4 lbs 9 oz rounded down to 4 1/2 lbs. Dosage 0.45 mL

Tidbit — 2 lbs 11 oz rounded down to 2 1/2 lbs. Dosage 0.25 mL

## PLAN YOUR KITTENS' BIRTHDAY PARTY (pg 75)

1. If 4 feet of streamers, you need 4 packs.
If 3 feet of streamers, you need 5 packs.
2. You need 26 toy mice.
3. 720 feet
4. 11:40
5. 5 packs. You'll spend $13.75. $10 is not enough.
6. About 7 songs
7. 3 sticker sheets
8. 9 chocolate, 7 strawberry

## MAKE YOUR PARTY SCHEDULE (pg 76)

10:00 clean house
10:30 decorate
12:00 party — welcome guests
12:15 Pin the Tail on the Kitten
12:35 snacks
1:00 sing Happy Birthday, cut the cake
1:20 open kittens' presents
1:45 dance party!
2:15 hand out goody bags
2:30 guests leave
2:40 clean up
3:25 take a break
5:30 dinner

Your break is 2 hours 5 minutes

## HOW WILL YOU CUT THE BIRTHDAY CAKE? (pg 77)

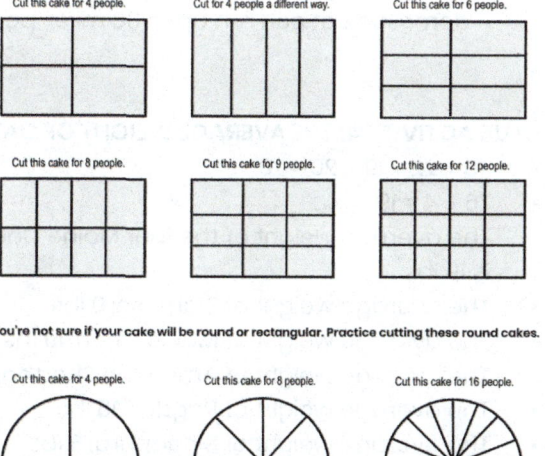

## CLUB ACTIVITY 1: EYE COLORS (pg 84)

- black kitten + green eyes
- black kitten + gold eyes
- black kitten + blue eyes
- brown kitten + green eyes
- brown kitten + gold eyes
- brown kitten + blue eyes
- orange kitten + green eyes
- orange kitten + gold eyes
- orange kitten + blue eyes

There are 9 different combinations.

## CLUB ACTIVITY 2: CAT SYMMETRY (pg 85)

## CLUB ACTIVITY 3: COOL CAT FACTS (pg 87)
- A female kitten can get pregnant as young as 4 months old.
- The oldest known cat, Creme Puff, lived to be 38 years old.
- Cats sleep an average of 15 hours per day.
- Cats can jump 5 times their own height.
- People began keeping cats as pets 9,500 years ago.
- Cats can make 20 different sounds that mean different things.
- A domestic cat can run up to 30 miles per hour.

## CLUB ACTIVITY 4: THE AVERAGE WEIGHT OF CATS (pg 88)
- 15 + 22 + 19 + 20 = 76
- 76 ÷ 4 = 19
- The average weight of the four Maine Coon cats is 19 lbs.
- The average weight of Siamese: 9 lbs
- The average weight of Maine Coon: 19 lbs
- The average weight of American Shorthair: 10 lbs
- The average weight of Ragdoll: 15 lbs
- The average weight of Singapura: 6 lbs

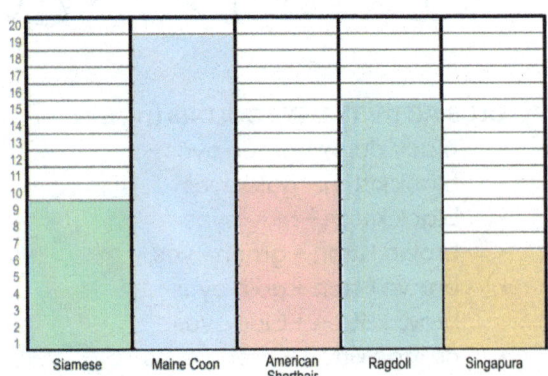

## CLUB ACTIVITY 5: THE ORANGE CAT GAME (pg 91)

- Smallest to largest: Singapura, Siamese, American Shorthair, Ragdoll, Maine Coon
- On average, a Ragdoll is 6 lbs bigger than a Siamese
- On average, a Siamese is 1 lb smaller than an American Shorthair
- On average, a Maine Coon is 13 lbs bigger than a Singapura
- The average weight of all 20 cats is a little over 11 lbs (236 ÷ 20)
- If you have just a few cats, even one extra large or extra small cat can make the average seem bigger or smaller than it really is. With more cats, you are more likely to get more examples of cats at the normal weight for that breed.

# GAME BOARDS AND CUT-OUTS

You can also download and print these online when you sign up at:
**artfulmath.com/kitten2-goodies**

- **Rounding X's**
- **Integer Number Line**
- **Fraction Cats**
- **Kitten Blanket Game**
- **Pin the Tail on the Kitten**
- **Make a Kitten Toy Schedule**
- **Feet and Inches "Bump"**
- **Kitten Purr-sonality Words**
- **Furniture Cutouts**
- **Certificate of Achievement**

# ROUNDING X'S GAME BOARD

Player 1

| 0.1 one tenth | 0.2 two tenths |
|---|---|
| 0.3 three tenths | 0.4 four tenths |
| 0.5 five tenths | 0.6 six tenths |
| 0.7 seven tenths | 0.8 eight tenths |
| 0.9 nine tenths | 1.0 one whole |

Player 2

| 0.1 one tenth | 0.2 two tenths |
|---|---|
| 0.3 three tenths | 0.4 four tenths |
| 0.5 five tenths | 0.6 six tenths |
| 0.7 seven tenths | 0.8 eight tenths |
| 0.9 nine tenths | 1.0 one whole |

You can download and print this page online at **artfulmath.com/kitten2-goodies**

## INTEGER NUMBER LINE

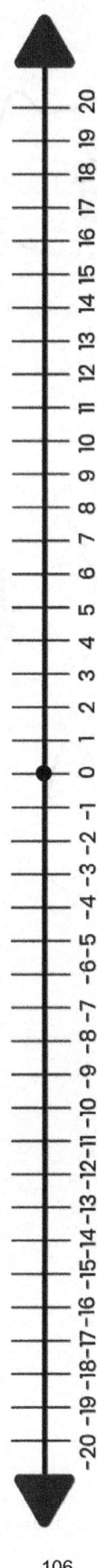

You can download and print this page at
artfulmath.com/kitten2-goodies

# FRACTION CATS GAME BOARD

# KITTEN BLANKET GAME BOARDS

PLAYER 1

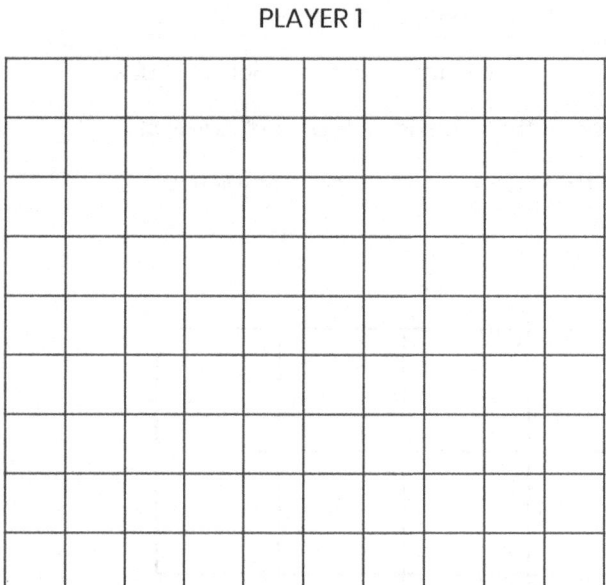

PLAYER 2

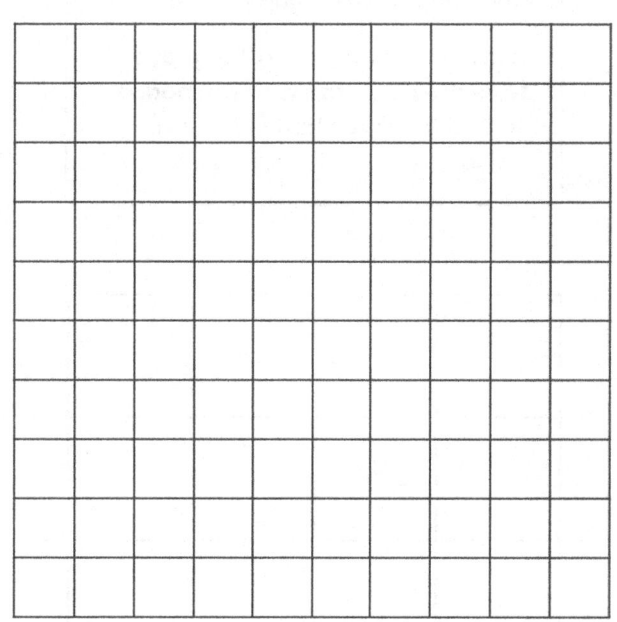

PLAYER 3

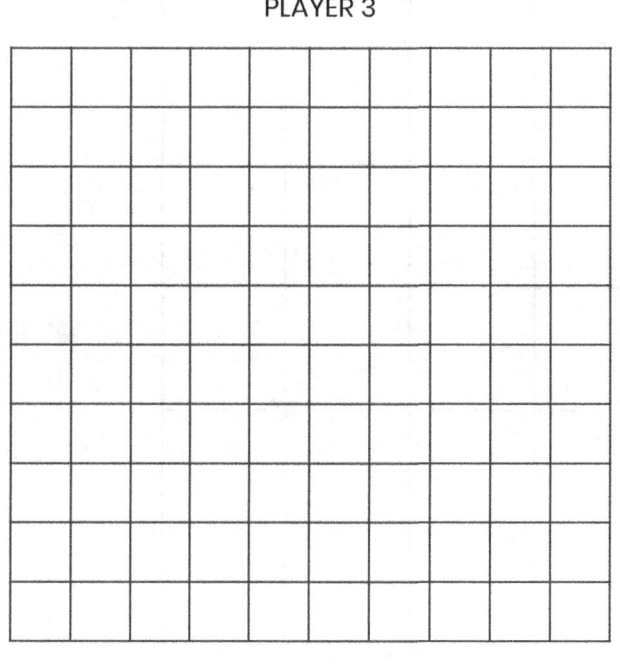

PLAYER 4

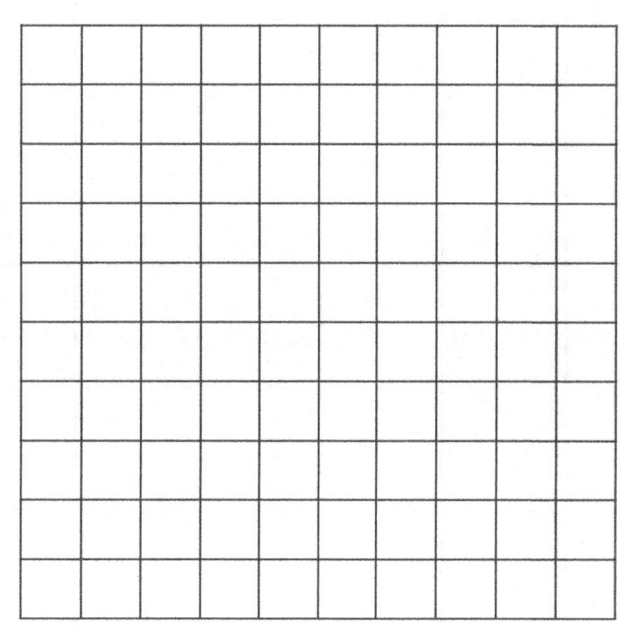

You can download and print this page online at **artfulmath.com/kitten2-goodies**

# PIN THE TAIL ON THE KITTEN - GAME BOARD FOR THE "HIDER"

Cut out the kitten on page 112. Give the tail to the Guesser.

**Without showing the other player, tape the kitten to the game board** so that the kitten butt (X) is at a place where two lines cross.

1. The **guesser will say a number pair,** like 2, 8. (Coordinate numbers go ACROSS, then UP.)
2. If any part of the kitten is on that spot, say **PURR**.
3. If no part of the kitten is on that spot, say **HISS**.
4. If the kitten butt X is on that spot, say **MEOW!**

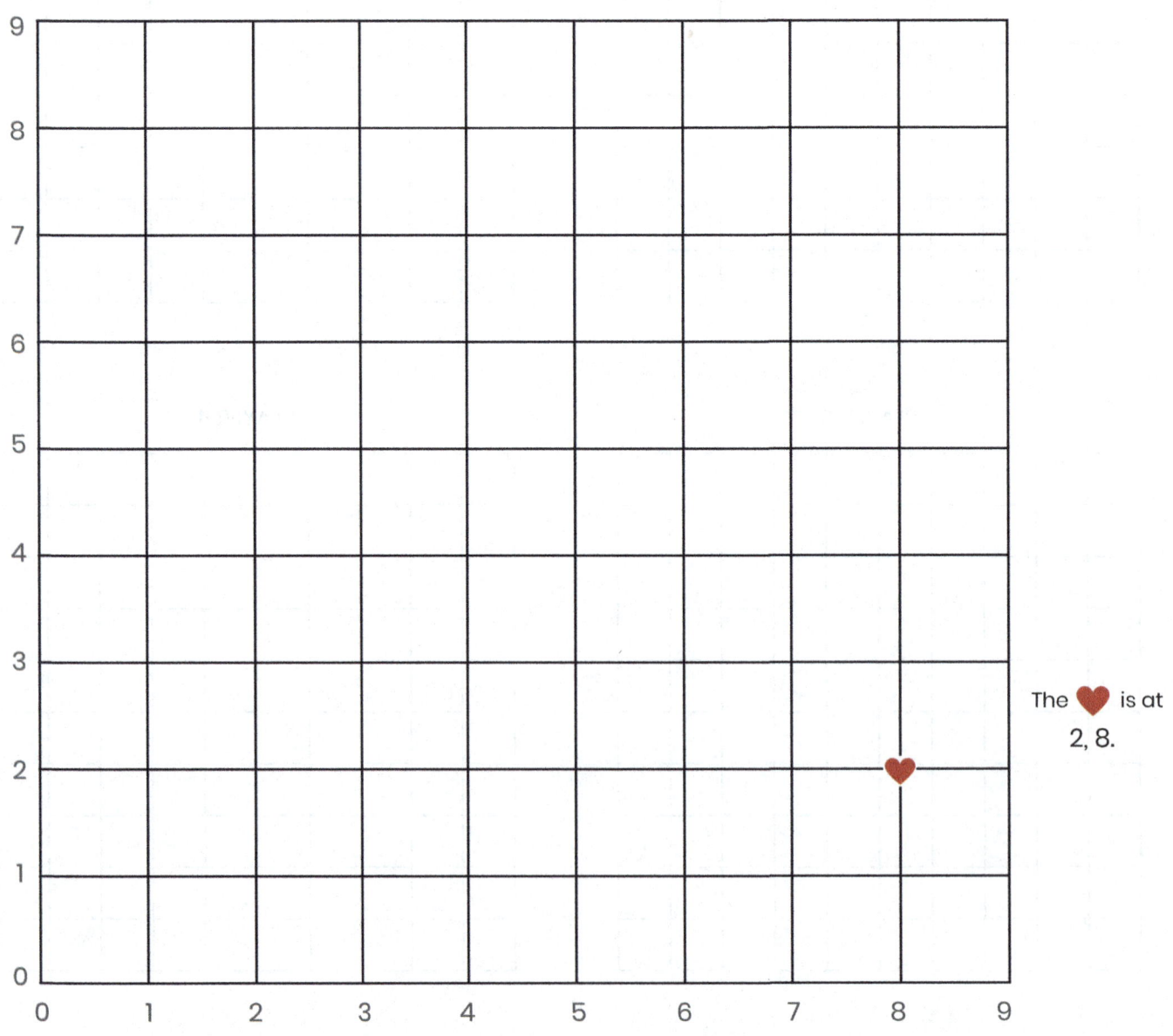

The ♥ is at 2, 8.

You can download and print this page online at **artfulmath.com/kitten2-goodies**

# PIN THE TAIL ON THE KITTEN - GAME BOARD FOR THE "GUESSER"

- Take the **kitten's tail** from page 112.
- **Guess** where the kitten is hiding. Try to find where the tail goes.
- Say the two numbers that mark that spot, such as "2, 8". (Read the numbers ACROSS, then UP.)
- If your guess lands on the kitten is, your partner will say **PURR**. Draw a DOT where the two lines cross.
- If your guess misses the kitten, your partner will say **HISS**. **Draw an X** where those lines cross to show your kitten is not there.
- When you guess exactly where the tail goes, they'll say **MEOW!**
- **Tape the tail** to the kitten on the other player's board. You did it!

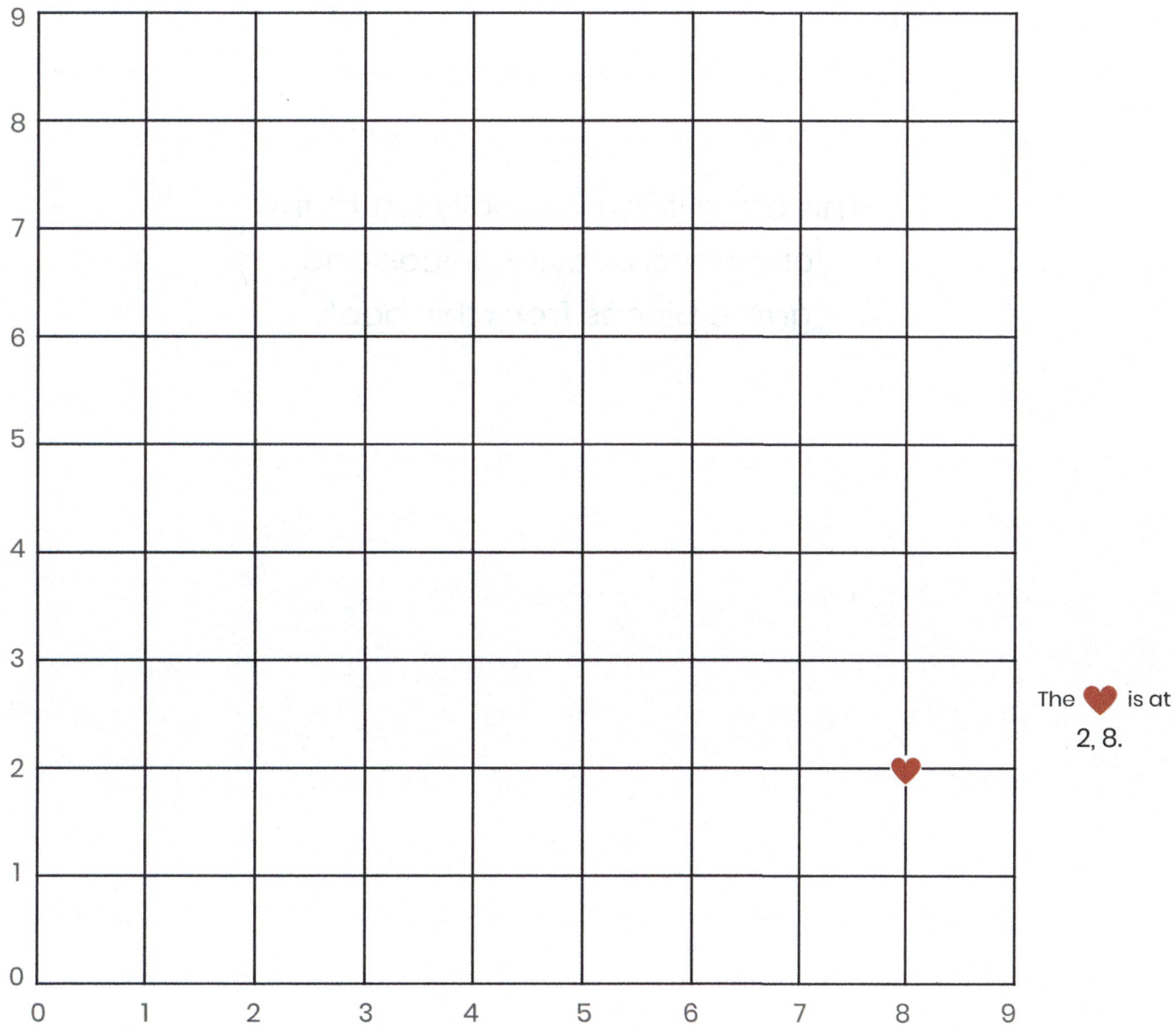

The ♥ is at 2, 8.

You can download and print this page online at **artfulmath.com/kitten2-goodies**

This page is intentionally left blank
for cutting activity pieces and
game pieces from this book.

# PIN THE TAIL ON THE KITTEN

**Cut out the kitten and its tail** to use with the game on page 81.
Give the BODY to the person hiding the kitten. Give the TAIL to the person looking for the kitten.

You can download and print this page online at **artfulmath.com/kitten2-goodies**

This page is intentionally left blank
for cutting activity pieces and
game pieces from this book.

# MAKE A KITTEN TOY SCHEDULE

Cut out the words below to help solve the puzzle on page 50.

| play mat | tunnel | puzzle toy | crinkle toy | mouse |
|---|---|---|---|---|
| puff ball | spring | wand toy | jingle ball | kicker toy |

You can download and print this page online at **artfulmath.com/kitten2-goodies**

This page is intentionally left blank
for cutting activity pieces and
game pieces from this book.

# FEET AND INCHES BUMP GAME BOARD

| 1 | 127 inches |
| 2 | 76 inches |
| 3 | 56 inches |
| 4 | 21 inches |
| 5 | 47 inches |
| 6 | 35 inches |

| 7 | 46 inches |
| 8 | 69 inches |
| 9 | 52 inches |
| 10 | 161 inches |
| 11 | 180 inches |
| 12 | 130 inches |

You can download and print this page online at **artfulmath.com/kitten2-goodies**

This page is intentionally left blank for cutting activity pieces and game pieces from this book.

# KITTEN PURR-SONALITY WORDS

Cut out the words below to use in the activity on page 25.

| silly | shy | sweet | cuddly | playful |
| brave | calm | affectionate | | confident |
| persistent | | stubborn | funny | social |
| easygoing | | adventurous | | opinionated |
| talkative | | energetic | happy | curious |
| crazy | wild | independent | | careful |
| content | | fearless | quiet | smart |
| sensitive | | goofy | full of surprises | |
| loyal | friendly | | mischievous | protective |
| daring | | loving | bossy | gentle |

You can download and print this page online at **artfulmath.com/kitten2-goodies**

This page is intentionally left blank
for cutting activity pieces and
game pieces from this book.

# FURNITURE CUTOUTS: DESIGN A CAT-FRIENDLY HOME

This page is intentionally left blank
for cutting activity pieces and
game pieces from this book.

**Cut out the images below.** You will use them to design your cat-friendly home!

You can download and print this page online at **artfulmath.com/kitten2-goodies**

This page is intentionally left blank
for cutting activity pieces and
game pieces from this book.

**Cut out the images below.** You will use them to design your cat-friendly home!

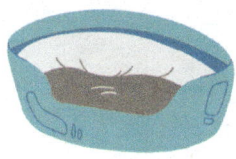

You can download and print this page online at **artfulmath.com/kitten2-goodies**

This page is intentionally left blank
for cutting activity pieces and
game pieces from this book.

Made in the USA
Monee, IL
10 September 2025

24576230R10077